CROATOAN

PART I

In the Beginning

JAMES OLDS

Brilliant Books Literary
137 Forest Park Lane Thomasville
North Carolina 27360 USA

CROATAN

Reprinted with Permission, Historic Urban Plans, Ithaca, NY USA

In 1587, one hundred and seventeen men, women, and children set sail for Sir Walter Reilgh's third and final attempt to establish a permanent English settlement in the New World. They were destine to become the *Lost Colony*, leaving behind only the word *Croatoan* craved in a post.

History hath forged that which
eternity shall bind

Preface

I started writing this book, maybe not for the standard reasons that a man might write a book, but, you see most of the men that I have had the fortune or misfortune of knowing in my life seem to be uncomfortable in discussing, even in the most casual of terms this basic concept of love. Perhaps it infringes or their "concept" of manhood, or for a myriad of different excuses. But, I have come to learn that there is one simple fact in life, we all "seek" to find our own concept of love. Even this begs the question, "how do we, individualy, define love"? By this very question, I don't mean the "preverbeal one night stand" but rather the true definition of love as only our heart and our very soul can define. In my own personal quest I find that the 1990's Bryan Adams song "Everything, I do, I do it for you" probably professes everything I mean by love. All my life I have searched for "that one special person" that we could truly wrap or embrace this moniker on. After three marriages, which I am not proud of, each time I thought I had finally found true person. One, in fact after eight and a half years of marriage and two children, I came to find did not even know the color of my eyes. After another marriage, I truly felt that I had found that one "special" person that shared this feeling with me. This is the person that I started writing this book for. I actually started the first chapter over several times and perhaps the first chapter, as one reviewer told me "was rather academic" but I felt that it lead in was necessary to present the proper image or tone for the remainder of the book. But, to my dismay, when I actually got about halfway through, I presented it to "that one special person" as a "gift" thinking that she would find it as precious as I did and what I was hoping for. When she did not even open it under the excuse of "you know I don't read anything unless I have to", I began to understand that my search continued. It was not until I was diagnosed with MS (Multiple Sclerosis) and lost even the ability to stand, that I relized that my efforts over the years was all one sided. This shocking development did not come bursting on to the screen until late one night, around 3 AM to be more exact, that this presumably "the love of my life" attempted to murder me with a pillow over my face! Now, to an ordinary person this may not sound that bad but to a quadriplegic, this is just as threatening as a gun or knife! At any rate, all of that can be for a different discussion.

In an attempt to describe my own personal search for love, I chose a part of American history that I fear may be lost on many. As an ardent "student" of American history and native to the Tidewater region of southeastern Virginia, I have had a long fascination when it comes to the issue of the "lost colony." After numerous visits to the site, it appears to be most strange and intriguing that the colonists who were from the sixteenth-century urban England would place their strongest weapon, a ship's cannon, pointing out to sea, rather than inland to provide some form of defense against the presence of hundreds of Native Americans that most textbooks fail to mention.

At any rate, as the book suggests, my search for "true love" continues, even though I am now confined to a wheelchair. I hope you will enjoy reading this as much as I had in writing it!

CHAPTER ONE

...In the beginning

In the early years of the 1600's, typhoid placed a strangle hold on the fledging English settlement known as Virginia. During this dark period, an old woman, whom they had come to know as *Auntie Catherine* lay dying in her frontier home. Before her death she had sworn to tell the sordid tale of those that had become known as the *Lost Colonists*, amongst which were their parents...

"She's convulsing again", shouted Steven to his twin brother who was seated at a crude table not far away. As with all of the sparse appointments in this frontier cabin the table was made of a rough-cut pinewood lashed together with deer hide thongs. "Fetch me another blanket!"

Samuel picked up a nearby bear skin instead and approached his brother. "Don't have no more 'cept this here bear hide."

"That'll have to do, she's slippin' fast. This fever's got's to break!"

Both young men stood over the elder woman they had grown to know as *Auntie Catherine.* Each was deeply concerned for the woman who had raised them since the death of their parents. But each displayed this concern in a different fashion. Steven, the eldest of the two, possessed a more visible way of expressing his feelings, where Samuel appeared to be more reserved. It was this expression of concern that drove Steven to tend to the sick woman where Samuel retreated to his own reflections. While Steven attempted to nurse Auntie Catherine, Samuel was more content to clean his musket at the table. Some of the local folks took this difference to mean that Samuel was uncaring and cold hearted. But nothing could be farther from the truth. It was just the difference in emotions, one suppressed, the other expressed. This particular set of twins, in many ways, was a reflection of each other, opposite in every detail. One right handed, the other left; one serious, one carefree.

It had been so long that neither had clear memory their parents, only Auntie Catherine. She had always been there for them, and now she was on the verge of death, leaving them alone on the Virginia frontier.

The twins had lived here almost all of their possible eleven or so years. No one knew for sure what their true age was. No one on the frontier really cared about such things.

"What was she speakin' of" asked Samuel.

"I's knows not. She was babblin', delirious she is with fever. Don't take nothin' she says right now as gospel."

"She was ramblin' on 'bout royalty wasn't she?"

"Aye" responded Steven as he tucked in the corners of the bearskin around her.

Samuel reached over and touched her forehead. "Blimey, she's on fire!"

"Aye" responded Steven, "and her belly is covered with these redish-pink spots and swole up."

"You know brother" began Samuel, "yesterday I was talkin' to Manawetak. He was frightful worried fer Auntie."

"Well that crazy old medicine man has been sweet on her fer some time."

"Aye, ever since she made him that pumpkin bread. Well, at any rate he told me that he had this vision, see, back when he was treatin' a young brave who had a similar fever. He said that the spirit of the wood owl came to him during this vision, and told him that warmth is not what is needed, but cold."

Pulling back from his Auntie, Steven responded, "That's stupid. She's shakin' 'cause she's cold. She might be on fire, as you say, but she's shakin' from cold! That's why's ye got's to cover her up. And that me brother, is why they's savages and we ain't."

"He went on to say that the owl told him to make a tea of snakeroot and a dash of oil from a skunk. Git 'im to sip at it whilst ye place cool hog lard in an onion poultice on the chest." Samuel paused for a moment to see if his brother was even listening, which of course in his typical fashion he was not. He was much more engrossed in caring for Auntie Catherine and wiping her brow.

"Steven!" Samuel almost shouted to gain his attention. "The young brave that he was treatin' got better!"

"Hush, Sam" scolded Steven. "You'll disturb her!"

Samuel would not take no for an answer, however, so he grabbed his brothers arm and turned him around. Looking Steven straight in the eye Samuel said, "look brother, I love her too, but she's is certain to die tonight if we can't save her. You have tried everythin' you know, let's try somthin' new! Who knows?"

"Well", began Steven, looking back at his Auntie Catherine…"I guess we could try…but just a little…"

"Great" exclaimed Samuel. "Now take off those blankets and give me one. Whilst I's git's it wet and cold in the snow, you set in to makin' the poultice and tea."

The two young men, eager to save their Auntie by any means possible set out in their assigned tasks. Neither one knew what the night would hold, nor cared as long as their Auntie would be okay. As Samuel returned from outside with his cold soaked blanket, he could see that Steven was finishing his task of the tea. "Hurry up Steve", called Samuel to his brother.

Just as the words departed his lips, Catherine started to babble again. But this time she appeared more lucid, more aware of her surroundings.

"Remember your place me boys" she began. "It all started with history, history of the Royals and what they's did to our homeland. It began with the passing of the great one, the one named Henry…"

"Blimey Steven, she's at it again! Quick give's her the tea!"

Samuel cautiously wrapped his Auntie Catherine with the wet, cold blanket while his brother supported her head and administered the tea. The coolness of the blanket dissipated rapidly and sent her into yet another round of convulsions.

"Stop it Sam", shouted Steven. "I told you that she is already cold; see what you've done to her!"

"I know, I know, but it is what Manawetak told me would happen. He said this happens at first but keep doin' it until she stops. Look brother, this blanket was wet; her heat has made it dry that fast!"

"Well…okay, may be you're right, fetch another wet one Sam."

"Aye, I'll be right back! Git her to take all of that tea!" As Sam passed through the cabin door he asked, "Is the poultice ready?"

"Yea, I'll git's it."

Auntie Catherine started again babbling on about history and their need to know about the past. This time she started to talk almost as if she were conversing in separate tongues of a different sort, of a different people, or acting out some scene from an unseen play…then she slipped into an unconscious state as the two brothers continued their duties throughout the night.

As the night progressed, Samuel continued his drudgery and went out for more and more cold blankets until sleep deprivation and exhaustion began to take its toll. He had difficulty in concentrating on his task and soon he found his mind wandering. The Virginia country side was glistening on the crest of a new fallen snow. Their cabin was situated a days ride from Jamestown on the valley floor directly below the western foothills of the coastal plain. They had found the abandon cabin after his Maw and Paw had passed and did their best to live in harmony with the natives.

It was, for the most part, a peaceful valley with a small stream flowing through it. Reaching it was but just a short walk from the cabin. The temperature was not yet quite cold enough to freeze the stream, but he knew the time was coming where he could soon walk across it. Blimey, he thought to himself, *snows come earlier this year. Trees just dropped their leaves! We's need to gets some meats stored and fast fer winter… wonder how late it be?*

He looked skyward, and through the barren tree branches he could see the stars above. The night was clear and held the distinct crispness of coming winter. The stars above gave light to the earthly objects below, illuminating his path. Manawetak had told him that the local natives believed that when a person died their soul was cast skyward and reflected in the stars above. *I wonder if Maw and Paw are there,* he thought quietly, *shinin' down all twinklin' like.*

He collected the blanket from the stream and started back towards the cabin. After taking only a few steps back towards the cabin he heard a scream. It was a blood-curdling scream! It was his Auntie!

"The King is dead!" She screamed. "The King is dead!"

Samuel raced back to the cabin, wet blanket in tow. Upon reaching the cabin door, he threw it open. When he did, he saw his Auntie sitting up in the crude bed. She had both hands on the shoulders of Steven and she was shaking him violently.

"The King is dead!"

As Samuel entered the room, Steven saw him and called out, "Sam, help me gits her back into bed!"

The two young men struggled with their Auntie, who despite her advanced age was capable of putting up quite a resistance. But youth soon prevailed and they soon were able to get her to lie back down. Samuel place the cool blanket back over her as Steven replaced the poultice that had come free in her struggles.

"What happened?" Samuel asked of Steven.

"I's told you, she's delirious with fever. She don't knows what's she's doin'. I's don't think that yer idea of the cold is helpin' much."

Sam reached over and placed one hand on her forehead. "What do ya mean? Her skin is near normal."

Pushing his brother away Steven said, "Let me see!" As he reached out and touched her he remarked in wonderment, "Blimey, yer right!"

Within another hour or so, Auntie Catherine regained consciousness. In a raspy voice the old woman called out, "boys? Are you here?"

"Aye Auntie, I am right here besides you."

"Who is that? Is that you Steven?" And she reached out trying to touch him.

He quickly grabbed her hand and guided it towards his face. "I'm right here Auntie, have been all night."

"Bl—bless you child" she responded with a hoarse cough and spit out blood. "I knew you would be here". Struggling to continue to speak the old woman asked, "Where is yer brother?"

"I'm here too Auntie. Me and Steven We's both cared fer ye all night. You's had us worried there fer a bit."

"I'm 'fraid child that it's over fer me" coughed Catherine. And again she passed a large thick globule of blood. "Come's sit down 'side me and let me looks at both ye."

The two young men did as instructed. However each knowing deep within, yet finding the revelation too disturbing to voice, that despite their efforts, this may be the last time with their beloved Auntie. *She has the haze 'bout her*, Steven thought to himself as he sat listening.

"I've seen the angel of darkness at me bedside" she began. "I's know it ain't long 'fore I's pass."

"No Auntie, you can't" cried Samuel. "Manawetak said you would be okay, like the young brave he helped!"

She mustered the strength and reached up to brush his hair away from his eyes. "This old body's worn, child. I's 'fraid I'll be gone 'fore daybreak. 'Fore I's pass, ye need to know of yer parents" Auntie Catherine coughed again.

"We already know" said Samuel. "The others in town told us that Mom died a witch and Paw as the Heretic that loved her. That's why they don't want us in town Auntie."

"No child" Auntie responded in her calming sort of way, and patted his hand amidst coughing up yet even more blood.

"That's not true. That's only what the ignorant say, cause they's don't understand…and they's fear what's they's don't know" replied Catherine coughing even more. "All she was doin' was practicing a ritual that she picked up when we was in New Spain, at a place called Saint Augustine."

"New Spain! I have heard of that place, south of here for many days! The Spanish hate us! Why were you and Maw there" questioned Samuel excitedly.

"Oh shut up Samuel" replied Steven in defense of his Auntie. And gave his brother a swat with the back of his hand. "You are disturbing her and she don't have to explain nothin' to the likes of you!"

"That's okay child" Catherine reassured Steven. "My time draws near and you need to know the truth, such as it is. Your mother was not a witch, this I know for certain. And yer father's only crime was to love her deeply and unconditionally. His love fer her, was somewhat hidden, however. In a lot of ways he was like you Samuel."

Samuel looked surprised at the suggestion, and gave a sly smile to ward off the charge and as if he were innocent of some falsely accused crime.

"Oh, I's know you's want every one to think you are some big tough woodsman…but" she said with a struggled smile despite her inner pain, yer Auntie knows you to be different." With these words she drew in a shallow, yet much need breath. Breathing was becoming increasingly more difficult for her as mucus seeped into her lower lung cavity. After this short pause she continued, "His love for her was much like those stories you two enjoy so much, from the Good Book. Your father's love for her was total, all consuming and everlasting. It drove him across the ocean after a four year separation. It caused him to set off into the frontier, into New Spain and fight with the Devil himself!"

Both Steven and Samuel exchanged glances, both were wondering if she was slipping back into delirium again, yet she continued.

"I's knows what yer thinkin'. I sees it in yer eyes…you think yer old Auntie is loosin' it…don't ya?"

The question seemed to hit surprisingly hard for the two lads as they exchanged quick glances with each other trying not to be seen by their beloved Auntie. The silence of the night hung over them like a blanket until finally Steven spoke. "No Auntie, we thinks yer fine…cept …cept that before you… you was out of it with fever." He twirled his finger around on the blanket covered bed with his head hung low out of a self-perceived form of shame as he spoke.

Catherine lifted her frail hand and stroked his blonde, matted hair in a calming fashion to brush away his despair. She knew what this night must be like for these two. She knew, deep in her heart, that this simple beginning of her story was already confusing them, for most of their parents life had remained an enigma for them. "Come close you two, for my time is short and I will tell you my last story."

For years, all their life it seemed, their Auntie Catherine was there for them…always the story teller, educator and counselor. Now, to face life without her, well… the prospect of such was too much for the brothers to bear and to think about it, brought tears to their eyes. Each drew near as she had asked and they settled in for comfort, more for their own rather than hers, but they knew that their nearness, although crowded her, brought on a reassurance that she would not part from.

"This story" she began, "starts with what me own Grandma told me. She, at one time, was employed in the Royal Laundry, for Henry VIII. She had a great love for stories about the Royals and would entertain the others in the laundry with their tales. She was particularly fond of tales about King Henry and considered him to be the main one that created the future for England. Her name was Anne. She took it particularly hard, although she worked just as hard not to show it when he passed. She was on duty there, in the laundry the day he died…

As she unveiled her story, a story that she alone contained within her, the words took on a life of their own as if painting a scene before their young eyes.

"The King is dead, that is for certain."

Anne stopped her scrubbing duties for a moment and looked at her friend on the other side of the washbasin. She could tell that her friend was tired, probably from yet another late night episode. She wasn't really much to look at, but that did not seem to discourage her men suitors. "You know Rachel, you needs to slow down a bit, 'fore it's too late. You could end up with somethin' you's don't want…like a husband."

Laughing, she continued with her duties, but then interjected "What do you mean, Rachel?"

"I's say, the King is dead!"

Again Anne paused. As she stood there looking blankly at her friend she began to hear the wailing of the nursemaids as the sound reverberated down the stone hallways. The scent of burning incense, long a Catholic tradition that had been carried over to the *new establishment* was barely detectable over the lye soap of the laundry. "Then why 'm scrubbin' his clothes" she exclaimed with a smile. "Ye didn't have something to do with his passin', did ye?" Anne asked of her friend. For it had been well known amongst the ladies of the Royal Laundry that Rachel was no stranger to Henry's bed.

Blushing, Rachel sheepishly retorted, "why's no in that case he's been dead for sometime he has."

With her answer the two young women laughed out loud, much to the scowling of the Head Laundress.

"All's rights you two, game times over!"

Speaking softly so she could barely be heard, Rachel replied, "Blasted witch! Guess we best be movin' on."

So they attempted to continue their duties as they worked hard on the scrub boards. In time, their laughter had turned to giggles.

Anne eventually broke the merriment with, "I guessin' the Lords will be glad, they didn't like 'im much."

"Aye," responded Rachel. "But what 'e did fur the rest of us, he'll be blessed for it."

Rachel reminded her friend that the passing King's reign had set the stage for the most magnanimous course of events in

Anglican history. For under his reign, Henry had set in motion those events that would permeate through the very heart of society. He transformed feudal England into a society were mere peasants could rise above their ancestor's status through hard work and ingenuity. His enclosures issue was just one of such events. This particular *issue* brought an end to the feudal Lords control over the countryside and the subsequent traditional arrangements for the raising of herds. Simply put, it allowed for the fencing in or hedging of open ranges upon which the poor had relied upon for their livelihood. Herding of sheep within fenced areas was considered by the landowners to be much more efficient than that of open ranges and cattle. This "re-shaping" of English country displaced the peasantry often to the cities.

"That Henry, he was a dirty one" remarked Anne as she held up a pair of his under shorts.

"Is you referring to the man or his shorts?" asked Rachel.

"Either one, look what he did to his first" said Anne referring to Henry's first wife, Katherine.

"Aye, but me brother is now a Journeyman in silver. He couldn't do that before." With that, both ladies continued silently with their duties.

The changes that Henry instituted in the simple life of the peasants had a long-lasting affect on the English economy, but nothing could match his efforts to produce a male heir. To this end one simple act to modern man but a devastating or a cataclysmic event to 16th century mankind was Henry's divorce of his first wife Katherine of Aragon.

"Wasn't she from Spain or somethin' like that" Rachel asked Anne.

"Who you askin' 'bout?" Anne asked inquisitively of her friend.

Rather disgusted, Rachel responded sharply as she laid down the clothing she was scrubbing. "I'm askin' 'bout His First! What was her name…?"

"Well", Catherine started to say but was interrupted by yet another body shaking coughing spree that culminated with yet another bloody globule being expelled from deep within her lungs. Regaining her composure once more, she continued…

"Anne, you see she was me Grand mum, and was a great follower of the Royal family and had long prided her self in knowing all the dirty details. She often would share the latest gossip with the others in the laundry. It served nicely as a means to pass the time. "Aye", responded Anne. "Katherine was the daughter of the famous Ferdinand and Isabella of Spain. She was first married to Henry's older brother Arthur, don't you know. But after only six months of marriage Arthur died without ever consummating the union."

"So" added Rachel, "he was a snake even then, marrying the wife of his dead brother, sounds like old Henry!"

"Aye", continued Anne "but that's why his father did what he did. Henry VII was rather reluctant to wed his only living son to this same woman. So he just let Katherine to stay on as his guest and function as the Spanish Ambassador to Court. Katherine filled this capacity for two years, supported rather frugally by Henry until he died. Some say that only her pride and arrogance sustained her during those years at court. With the passing of Henry VII, of course his son became King. This new King Henry was long enthralled with the tall, graceful Spanish blonde and married her within two weeks of his father's passing."

Snickering at the thought, Rachel interjected "Henry knew how to always get his way, he did."

"Aye", replied Anne.

"Tell me more Anne. I hear though that they did not last long as a couple."

"That's not really true" responded Anne. "In the early years of partnership theirs was a lovin' union. Both had similar interests in huntin', dancin', and intellectual discussions." Anne paused for a moment to catch her thoughts. "After a while, they's got's disappointed though after several miscarriages or stillbirths. Henry's love for her, however, appeared to be unadulterated. Some even said that Henry was often overheard saying *we are both still young, the sons will soon follow.*" After a while one child did survive, a daughter to whom the name Mary was given."

"That's the older Princess isn't it", questioned Rachel. "I hear she is still a Catholic."

"Aye but let me finish me story", exclaimed Anne as she splashed water at her friend and continued droning on about the Royals.

"Katherine's position remained steadfast. When Henry went overseas to fight in France, Katherine was appointed Governor of England."

"Blimy!" remarked Rachel, "she shore rose up fast!"

"Aye, and during her tenure, English troops defeated the Scots at the Battle of Flodden and succeeded in killing the Scottish monarch."

"She was the one responsible for that too?" questioned Rachel.

"Aye" Anne responded. "She united the Kingdom once again. Then, based on her Spanish heritage, alliances were renewed between our two countries.

Despite her successes, Henry was not to give up his pursuit of the male heir. As time dragged on disappointment followed disappointment and Katherine was soon perceived as unable to produce the much-demanded male heir. This, in turn, caused much dissention at Court. So, Henry sought *relief* in the arms of other women, one of which mothered his illegitimate son, Henry, Duke of Richmond."

"The Duke! Why I ever would have guessed it?" said the astonished Rachel. "Go on Anne, this is getting good!"

Smiling even more, Anne continued her story. "Solidified in the opinion that Katherine was incapable of producin' the much-desired male heir, eventually Henry raised the specter of divorce. A divorce, particularly one of such magnitude, would have to be approved by the Pope, don't ye know, considering that the *world* was still Catholic and all that. Katherine, always the sharp operator, used her influence as Aunt to the Emperor of the Holy Roman Empire and successfully defeated Henry's repeated attempts to have the marriage dissolved. If she were unsuccessful, you see, it would have named their only child of the union, Mary, a bastard. Responding in kind, Henry committed the unthinkable and broke with the Church."

Rachel had stopped her chores sometime ago and had taken a seat on a near by stone. Stunned by what she had just heard Rachel was now in obvious disbelief. "How could he do that to her? She sounded like a good and God-fairing woman to me."

Continuing on with her story Anne had now attracted others in the laundry and she soon had a small gathering. "When He broke with the Church He made his own. Thus creatin' the Church of England with the King, himself at the head" Anne explained with a swish of her hand.

"That bloody bastard! You mean to tell me that our church, the Church of England is all because he wanted a divorce!"

"Aye! Removing the Pope from the picture, Henry was free to divorce Katherine and marry Ann Boleyn, his new love. That was number two" explained Anne.

Finishing their washing chores the two took the heavy baskets of wet clothing over to the line to hang them out to dry.

"Well", said Rachel "that would explain why the two daughters don't like each other."

"Aye, it does," added Anne. "But there's more…

After a series of unsuccessful marriages, the great King now has died leaving his sixth wife, Catherine Parr the widow and destines for some Convent somewhere."

"Pity, I's always did like her", explained Rachel, "even though I was beddin' her husband!"

Laughing Anne replied, "Yea, and you have a poor way of showing how much you liked her!"

"Oh hush, continue on Anne this is too interesting! How many children did the old man finally have? Some say as many as ten!"

"Oh no, not that many" reasoned Anne. "Of all of his relations, Henry fathered only four children, of which only three are considered *successors*. Henry's last will and testament, I hear from this friend of mine in the Kitchen" reflected Anne "has passed the Crown to his only son Edward and his descendants."

"Edward!" shouted Rachel. "Blimey, that sickly little ten year old! What is he to do with a Kingdom!"

"Oh Rachel, your just mad because you can't go to bed with him" laughed Anne.

"Well," remarked Rachel as she twisted some of her hair and swayed back and forth, "maybe I'll just wait and teach him. That is if he lasts long enough, as sick as he always is."

Snickering at the remark Anne playfully threw an article of clothing at her friend.

"**A**untie Catherine" questioned Steven as he interrupted her train of thought. "This is an interesting story and all, and I'm sure that your Grandmother was a good sort, but…"

Catherine looked over at him and she instinctively knew what the rest of his words were and so she took it upon herself to finish his thought. "You's wonderin' what all this has to do with yer Maw and Paw."

"Aye…I mean…its interestin' and all, but how does it connect?"

"Like most things lad, all things are connected and this story…" coughed Catherine… "The one from me own Grandma, set the scene for the play."

Both boys exchanged glances again. Samuel reached over and felt her forehead.

"She's burnin' up again, fetch more tea, I'll git another blanket!"

"I'll be fine", she responded aware of what was said. But it was too late, as both lads set off to complete their self-appointed duties.

When they returned and started to tend to their Auntie, she continued. "Life is much like a play that you would see or read about from those borrowed books. Life, all life has meaning and the pieces connect, even when the connection is not known. My Grandma would say what went on from King Henry started the entire English world. And, eventually those acts brought us together and to these shores."

Finishing their duties and at the same time allowing themselves to come to the realization that maybe she was okay and really had a message, the two brothers sat back down on the edge of the bed. Fluffing her pillow to provide additional comfort, both settled back in for the story as their Auntie Catherine continued. Her continuation of a story that was certain to change their life...

 . . . Just as predicted, Edward died six years later. The Crown, by Henry's will, was then passed to Mary, the only living offspring of Katherine and Henry's eldest daughter. Again, as before, the Crown was to be passed to her decedents, providing that she had any. Being raised a Catholic and daughter of Katherine, who had been ill-treated by the proper "English" church, Mary took as husband Prince Philip, a Hapsburg, of Spain.

As was customary in those days most royal families were related and inter married. This was no exception between Mary and Philip. Philip, younger than Mary by some considerable amount, was the son of Charles, Emperor of the Holy Roman Empire, who was the nephew of Katherine, Mary's mother.

Philip was heir to the Spanish throne. Spain was the undisputed ruler of the known world and whose empire, in its own right, extended from the Dutch colonies in the north to the Ottoman Empire in the south, including the rich holdings in New Spain. He saw it as his duty to extend the reign of Catholicism throughout the world, including bringing the rouge-state of England back into the fold. This was high on his list. Marriage to Mary was of convenience to bring this to fruition. Philip's plan was thwarted, however when the English Parliament refused to name him *King* based on his union with Mary.

Thus, Queen Mary ruled England with Philip by her side. Her reign was also short-lived for it only lasted five years until her own death in 1558. During this brief time religious upheaval and dissension ruled the day throughout much of Western Europe. Mary's union with Philip aligned England in Spain's war with France. This union served England's interests as well for France was aligned with Scotland against England. However, in the end Mary's reign saw the disillusion of the English claim to the northern coast of France with the fall of Caláis after nearly two hundred years of occupation.

Further, Mary attempted to undo all the religious reforms enacted by her father at the expense of her mother. Those loyal Protestants to the Church of England were rounded up by the hundreds and burned, thus earning the monarch the title as "Bloody Mary".

Mary's passing was without the creation of her own lineage and brought to the Throne Elizabeth, who was her half sister and daughter of Henry's second wife Anne. Elizabeth, like Mary, was staunchly religious, but to the Protestant movement and to the Church of England. After all it was this Church that she was raised and was created for her mother. Under Elizabeth's reign the Church of England was officially established with Protestant dogma, but liturgy and rites remained along the Catholic model. Shrewd to play the game of politics and forever the procrastinator, Elizabeth repeatedly delayed her decision to wed the persistent Philip, former husband to her older half sister. Philip, now King Philip II of Spain, was even more steadfast in his resolve to bring England back into the fold of Catholicism. Tensions grew between the two countries all the while Philip attempted to pursue Elizabeth's hand.

Spanish influence grew throughout the known world. Its coffers swelled with the enormous amounts of gold and treasure from the New World. This ever-increasing power and wealth brought the specter of a shift in the balance of power in Europe. Spain with its vast holdings was in a position where it could project its influence around the world. This situation did not bode well for Elizabeth's concept of England and its rightful place on the world stage. Additionally Elizabeth saw as her duty to bring a sense of calm back to her country after so many years of strife.

English support of the Protestant rebels in Denmark, which were fighting against the encroachment of the Spanish Empire, was expensive now that it was an open affair. Realizing the key to becoming a *world-class* power and society meant also building a Navy; which to do so Elizabeth found it convenient to siphon off some of this Spanish wealth from the New World. By doing so it would help keep Spain in check and not alter the balance of power dramatically. At the same time it would help provide funding for the expensive efforts in Denmark and the building of a Navy that was required to step out on to the world stage. To this end she commissioned two very able-bodied seamen, Francis Drake and his cousin John Hawkins.

Rising up on one elbow, Steven interrupted again. "Auntie Catherine, excuse me but…"

Before Steven was able to finish his sentence, Samuel jumped in. "Hush Steven!" he said with a stern frown. "Let Auntie finish!"

With a struggled smile, Catherine continued…

"Both men", she began amidst coughing, "had a deep hatred for the Spanish. Several years prior, both men had almost lost their lives after they were defeated in battle by the Spanish and sent a drift in open waters.

Eventually, after this stunning defeat they made their way back to the Caribbean. Drake and Hawkins quickly became familiar with the local waters and islands from which they enlisted the assistance from a few escaped African slaves that they found there…Soon they started to pray on the unsuspecting Spanish ports and gold shipments. However, despite his best efforts, their string of victories was not compensation enough for Elizabeth.

The Spanish vessels were very large; enormous actually, especially when compared to Drake's fleet of small, swift ships. Not being able to outgun the Spanish fleet, Drake had relied upon the swiftness and maneuverability of smaller vessels to overcome his lumbering prey. This decision, although successful in the attack, had a down side. With such small ships, Drake could not accommodate all of the gold and therefore his operation was not as efficient as the Queen wished it to be."

Calling him in for an accounting of his in-efficiency, the Queen summoned Drake to Hampton Court. She was to receive him in her normal fashion, in the throne room. Drake assumed this was more for formality and intimidation purposes than anything else. It did have its just affect.

Arriving just on time at Hampton Court, Drake looked around him as he entered the room. The room was enormous! The ceiling rose to a peak in the center and a good 50 feet from the floor. From the top there were tapestries depicting the various heroic events of English history. There were tapestries depicting the Crusades and the fall of Jerusalem, the defeat of the Scots at Flodden, ridding the land of the Saxons, the legendary Arthur, and his knights, from which all English monarchs attempted to trace their own personal lineage. The Battle of Hastings was depicted on yet another. The flying buttresses that supported this ceiling were of carved English Oak topped with the royal symbol of the lion's head on each. The floor was that of inlaid oaks, maple, and mahogany which presented a mosaic pattern and highly polished. Elizabeth herself was as stunning as ever! Her crisp white ruffled collar ringed her throat as if her head were on a linen draped tray. Her skin was snow white, adorned with pursed ruby lips, and shaved gold leaf danced throughout her hair, which was done up in a tight knot behind her. Drake gave a short half smile as he brought her into focus from across the room. When he saw the gold leaf in her hair, he knew that he was not in as much trouble as he originally thought. The gold leaf had been his *special present* from his last plundering mission. As he approached he realized why so many of his countrymen were willing to die for her kingdom, for she was to die for!

"Enter Francis Drake, advance and be recognized by your Queen!" bellowed the command.

Marching forward to within the prescribed ten feet from the lower step that ascended to the throne, he took a knee on his left and raised his glided sword hilt to his forehead as he bowed his head forward. "Your Majesty what is thou bidding?"

"You, Francis Drake have wasted precious time. It is you that convinced me to support this adventure of yours. Although your actions are noble and have brought us much treasure, when I consider what it takes to equip you and your men, the sum is not enough to offset the risks to the Realm. It, Mr. Drake, is only a matter of time that Phillip is no longer clouded by his proposed affection and seeks retribution. I suggest, Drake that if you cannot find a way to become more efficient in your deed, then I shall find another in your steed! Now rise and be off with you."

The Queen spoke these last words with a waving of her hand as if to shoe off an insect. Drake, realizing his plight, rose and departed quickly.

In another throne room on the other side of the continent, yet another monarch contemplated the future…

Philip, in the mean time grew increasingly more perplexed; how could this arrogant wench from a feudal blasphemous state continue to reject all the wealth and power the Spanish Throne had to offer? *After all,* he thought, *she was not even a legitimate heir, even for this lowly state of ill-clad clansmen!* Mary, the rightful heir had been his wife; therefore he should be King, or at least his appointee should sit on the Throne. After all, considering that the Pope, the only one who could grant a divorce, had refused to do so meant that Elizabeth's parents were not "properly" wed thus making her the bastard. Yet he cared for her maybe more so because she was the one thing he could not possess nor control. Her blasted support for the Protestant rebels in the Netherlands to the north and her refusal to bring the high sea raiders to justice further infuriated his wrath. These raiders had played on coastal towns in New Spain and raided Spanish gold shipments for nearly twenty years, and most recently, Saint Augustinè.

Now it was Samuel's turn to interrupt. "Hey, that's where you say you and Maw was!"

"Hush Samuel" replied Steven. "Let her finish!"

"It's okay Steven, at least"…Catherine started to say but then was interrupted again by more coughing. When the spell was over she picked back up in her story right where she had left off, as if the story was written down before her… "at least I know he's listening."

Taking a short breath the old woman continued with her story.

"Although she played the role well and smiled at his gestures, he knew that she was ultimately responsible.

Sitting alone one evening King Philip knew that something must be done to punish these sons of Satan and restore the order that was *Spain* to the world. He called for his advisors. "What news do you bring?" Philip bellowed as they entered the ornate room.

The room itself was larger than most cathedrals of the era. Originally built as a meeting hall for the Maids of Court, Philip, ever the scholar had turned it into a private library and reading room. It was only in here that Philip allowed decorations of any kind. Displayed around the room were art works from his vast personal collection, separated only by tapestries from central Europe, donated by his sister, who sat on the Hapsburg Throne. Shelving throughout the room was made from hand-carved oak, lining which were elements from his equally vast collection of rare books and prints. The ceiling was made from inlaid woods and precious metals from New Spain, interlaced with animal hide harvested from his holdings in the sub continent. The heavy English oak doors engraved with hunting scenes stood taller than four men, swung closed. *These had been a gift from her grandfather, Henry VII,* Philip paused to reflect.

"Your Excéllante, Spanish soldiers and subjects alike have been murdered, the peaceful port of Callo burned, and two ships sunk. One is reported to be the Nuestra Senora de la Conception" came the reply.

The attack on the port city was unsuccessful, but it gained Drake information, which he was able to track down the Spanish Galleon *Conception*, or *Cacafuego* (Fireball) as the sailors referred to her. The loss of the Galleon, however, was a different matter. This particular ship was of a newer design and especially developed to haul larger loads of treasure. In addition, the ship was armed heavier than others and therefore considered to be a more formable of an obstacle for these pirates to attack. The news was quite unsettling to the Spanish King. Attempting, however, to maintain his composure while in audience with this messenger, Philip felt it necessary to gain more details on the attack.

"Tell me is this all at the hands of these sea-born criminals from the north" Philip asked, although he knew the answer. His advisors would not report it this way if it were not so. To bring ill advice to the King was a sentence of death.

"Sé your exalted one" came the reply.

"And of the mission", Philip questioned?

"Our reports, your highness, indicate that the mission was burned and the villagers were taken, there is nothing left."

This infuriated Philip into a rage throwing his wine goblet across the room. Nervous servants quickly descended like insects upon the spill. Now these bandits had attacked and burned God's house! Sacred as a tomb and gateway to establishing the proper order of things in New Spain was the transformation of these simple pagan natives to the one true Church. "And the English Crown" asked Philip? "Pray good man what news? Does she do nothing?"

"Our spies' Highness tell us that she gives them safe harbor and it is reported that the English dungeons are the recruiting grounds for sailors. It is also said that her own coffers tax a hefty portion of what these bandits bring."

"How dare this wench flaunt her meager success against the might of Spain," cried Philip as he burst into rage and stormed about the room. "She is nothing more than a bandit herself, sneaking onto the throne the way she did. It is an outrage and a crime against civilized mankind to usurp the wishes of the "Church", boasted Philip. "Gather your sources and the admirals, send a messenger to the Emperor, I have had enough", exclaimed Philip! "We will see what this derelict country of clansmen is made of when they feel the full weight of Spain on their doors!"

Again Steven could not contain himself any longer. "Auntie Catherine, what's this got's to do with our folks? I mean I understand now why the Spanish hate us so, but I don't understand how this has anythin' to do with Maw and Paw… or why you's say you was in New Spain."

Catherine looked back at Steven and before she could respond her body erupted in a deep-chest coughing binge causing her to sit up straight on her bed. The horrible retching went on and on, until finally culminated in a horrendous up helve of bloody mucus.

"Steven!" cried Samuel. "Looks what's you did! You got's her all upset and the like. Just sit there and listen to her story… it don't matter!"

Attempting to regain her composure, she patted her own chest and slowly lay back down, reaching over to Samuel in reassurance. "I'm, okay Samuel, your brother did no wrong. His question was okay." Then turning her attention to both lads Catherine set out to explain why she had gone on the way she had about the Royals and Spanish. "You see lads", she began, "it was this setting, these actions, this time in our country's past that brought us all together. If you don't know the past, the future will make no sense…I thought I's taught you two that already"?

Steven, looking ashamed of his accusations was the first to respond, with his brother nodding in agreement. "Aye, Auntie, you did."

"Good" she said in acceptance. "Now, yer father was no Heretic, but he was what we used to call a street rat."

"First a Heretic, now a rat, great!"

"Steven, you must not judge that which you do not know" Catherine said in a scolding tone. "Times were hard, 'specially when one had no family and lived in the streets. We all's did things that we now wished we had not…even yer Auntie Catherine." With a heavy sigh she continued on with the story…

"A street rat is what we would call a thief that lived on their own, in the street and made their way in life off of others.

It was a life that most grew to know, cept the Royals. Them Royals just continued on in their way as if no one else was to matter; because no one did. But such was the world. Little did the average person know what events would transpire from this Royal Dance? The relations between monarch and monarch, bordered on foreplay at times would soon impact the seemingly bland lives of the innocent on both shores. These lives were nothing more than mere dust to either monarch and yet they would play decisive roles in the tumultuous events that lie ahead."

As Catherine continued, the brothers settled back down near her side. Here they would stay until the very end.

"Get back here you rouge," shouted the portly shop owner as he descended the staircase!

He had been abruptly woken to the sounds of an intruder. Still clothed in his nightshirt and cap he held the candle high so he could see past the glare of the flame. It was not yet sun up and the shadows of his dry goods stacked neatly around the store below offered excellent hiding for a would-be thief. Through the dim candlelight he could make out the slight figure of someone crouching behind some crates. Adjusting his sight for the darkness that still enveloped the shabby storehouse; the shop owner glanced around to ensure that there was only one potential intruder. As he looked around quickly, the images of his stores began to come into view.

Barrels of flour freshly milled on the continent, containers of salted fish and pork destine for the navy, cloth from the Far East that had minor flaws to the extent that the original owner had rejected the shipment and numerous others "like" items were plainly visible to his eye. He was proud of the store that he had built from the discarded items that came into the Customs House next door. As items came into the Customs House, they were sorted and taxed. If the shipment was not right for any reason, be it damaged in transit or the order filled incorrectly, the goods were returned to the shipper, and usually at the sea captains' expense. As a true capitalist, the shop owner had made a tidy business by capitalizing on others misfortune. Conveniently located next to the Customs House and sharing the adjoining warehouse and docking space, he would make an offer on these returned goods and then turn around and sell them as "seconds". This relieved the Customs House of an overstock and provided a means for the sea captains to recoup their own expense in transit.

Assuring himself that there was only this one intruder to concern himself with, he mustered his feeble courage. *These young lads,* "he thought, *must be reined in.*"

Infesting the wharf area as they had several months ago with their thieving ways had started to take its toll on his and everyone's business. He called out again, "you there, be off with you"!

Realizing that his cover was blown Tristan made for the door. Making his way down the staircase as best as possible, the Shoppe owner finally was able to make out the outlines of a figure. Through the dimly lit room he got a recognizable glimpse of the perpetrator. He recognized Tristan from before.

Calling out, "you there, I know you! You won't get away this time!"

Tristan, however, had different plans. Dashing away from behind the crates filled with fish and salt pork, he sprinted down the aisle. In hot pursuit, the shop owner followed. Tristan's youthful legs served him well, as they had for the past ten years of growing old on the streets of London. The shop owner was no match for Tristan's speed. Dodging the reaching grasp of the shop owner, Tristan made for the door.

Down the wharf he ran. He could see the torchlight of an early morning fishing crew ahead. The glow from their light cast an enchanting, yet eerie golden glow to the wet planks of the wharf. The shop owner attempted to follow, but Tristan was too fast. The shoppe owner was nearly forty, considered old in this day of age, but still had the stamina to pursue.

Calling out as he puffed down the wharf, "Thief! Stop him; Stop thief!" to anyone who would listen. "He stole my coin!"

Soon a Marine just coming on shift at the Customs House joined in. Now Tristan was in trouble! If he were caught now it would certainly mean the stocks! Although the Marine, a boy himself, was not much older, Tristan still had the advantage. Weighted down with musket, horn and the heavy woolen coat, the Marine was no match for Tristan's scarcely clad small frame. Around the containers of tea bound for the navy and through a collection of fishing nets and crates bound for sea, he ran.

"Stop, thief" shouted the Marine, "stop that boy!" The Marine shouted to the group of fishermen readying their nets for the day's catch, as Tristan dashed by.

"Hey, watch it you bilge rat", exclaimed one of the crusty old men as Tristan ran by. By torchlight the three men continued to work trying to finish their labors to start the day.

"'Onder what 'e did" one fisherman said to the other.

"On't knows but he sure can move, mind me of another day."

The older fisherman turned and said, "'ou ain't got that much 'nergy even for a woman!"

Laughing, the older man stood blocking the Marine's way.

"Make way for the Queen's duty!" shouted the Marine.

"The Queen?" was responded. "What She want with a scourge rat 'ike that one?"

"He's a thief you idiot", commanded the Marine, "Now make way!"

Stepping aside the fisherman turned to his mates and smiled then nudged a barrel containing apples, the contents of which spilled out onto the wharf, creating additional obstacles for the Marine. As the Marine struggled and made his way through the fruit, Tristan ran on into the early morning hour.

Turning left down a small alley Tristan made his escape to the street. Dodging carriages he ran across the cobblestones and quickly made his way to the blacksmith shop. Here he could find refuge!

"Smitty, quick where can I hide" shouted the breathless boy.

Smitty, always the early riser was already hard at work on his new contract work. "Aye lad what have you done now" replied the blacksmith as he pounded out the hot iron.

Smitty as he was known on the streets was fond of Tristan and employed his services from time to time to supplement his own meager income. Smitty had lost his wife giving birth to his own son years ago. For several years Smitty taught his own son the trade just as he had learned when the accident happened. Miscalculating the weight of the feed bags stored in the overhead rafters, Smitty's son Thomas was crushed when the beams gave way. Since then Smitty had not been the same, nor did he use the rafters for storage. Tristan had never met Thomas, but that did not bother Smitty, he still likes the lad.

"In there with the 'ourse feed" said Smitty. "'E won't find you there!"

"Smitty", exclaimed Tristan, "you didn't see me, okay?"

"You never mind me", Smitty said and he went back to his work. He had just earned a contract to repair and refit the rims on army carriages. It had taken six years to win this contract and Smitty was not going to jeopardize it! With this contract Smitty could actually hire an assistant and maybe pass his knowledge on to some deserving sole. *The boy? Maybe, but his thievin' ways would have to be concealed. It would be nice however;* Smitty mused, to have another son to pass the days with. Reflecting on the thought and a moment of pause, Smitty smiled and then shook his head as if to cast out the idea, and returned to his work of shaping the metal that would soon be a new rim.

Outside the clatter of Marines filled the streets. The sound of their hobbled boots on the street stones was worse than thunder itself to the pursued. Seven others, to include an equally young Lieutenant, eager to make his own name joined in pursuit.

"Good day, sir" announced Lieutenant Harvey Anson, as he marched into the blacksmith shop. He was a striking figure in his own right and well suited to the task of bringing law and order to the wharf.

"'Bout time you got 'ere", stated Smitty rather matter-of-factly as he dipped the newly caste rim in the cooling bath beside the anvil. Steam rose with a hissing sound that startled the young officer. This greeting confronted the young Lieutenant and caught him off guard. He was not expecting such, Smitty mused, "*Got him on the run, I do.*"

"Well just don't stand there gawking at me, where's me horse?"

"My good man", stammered the Lieutenant, "what are you speaking of?"

"*The voice was that of a fine noble from up-country*" thought Smitty. Not unlike the ones that had served in this manner for centuries. The Lieutenant had that *fresh* look to him, the one that stood in testimony to his lack of a hard life. He was a good six feet thought Smitty, certainly an upward mover to be at the Provost station at such an early age and rank. His red curly hair and the sprinkling of a few freckles gave him almost a school boy image, *definitely not from here*, thought Smitty. For the Lieutenant lacked the hardened look of someone from the city.

"The bastard ran in'ere, threatened me and 'tole me horse! He went out the side, to the street he did."

"Thank you sir" responded the Lieutenant, "your horse is as good as found."

Turning abruptly the young officer ordered his men to the pursuit. *Not today you won't,* thought Smitty.

The Marines departed to hasten their search in the streets. Once outside the Lieutenant called for the detail Sergeant. "Sergeant Billings!"

"Aye sir" came the response.

"I need you to post one of your men into the shadows to keep a keen eye on our livery friend. Something's amiss here, and I'm not sure what it is."

"In the shadows, sir" surprised that he had the nerve to question an officer, young or not, the good sergeant left the response hanging on the air. "Begging the sirs' pardon but sir, but did you say in the shadows" now trying to make his question of orders to seem more as a clarification.

"Yes Sergeant, in the shadows. Something is rotten in the State of Denmark", quoting the most recent play of the upstart play write, William Shakespeare. Lieutenant Anson had just viewed the play recently in the escort of the beautiful young daughter of the Regimental Commander. Lieutenant Anson was not overly impressed with the material of the play save this one line, which he used frequently. The evening, however, had been rather enchanting nonetheless.

"I need to know the comings and goings at this livery. From other events it seems to be some form of a hub. I have other business to tend to which will take me out of pocket for a tad. Carry on with the search and report back by mid morning. Remember this, not the means but only the ends must be honorable."

"Aye-aye sir", responded the sergeant smiling as he clicked his heels of his well polished boots together and rendered the appropriate salute. Commanding his marines, the Sergeant gave the order.

As his men departed, the Lieutenant turned and walked back to his quarters. "Now time to slip into my other clothes and have a meal. We shall see what we shall see" murmured the Lieutenant to himself.

Coming from behind the horse feed, Tristan stuck out his head. "Thanks mate" Tristan said "'ere something for the trouble", tossing him a small bag of shillings, one of several that he had pinched from the shopkeeper earlier. "I'll take you up on the 'orse offer", jumping on the closest mare, Tristan rode out the front and down the cobblestone street, dashing onto the main thoroughfare.

Making his way through the streets, which were unusually crowded for this time of the morning, Tristan arrived back at his *hole* as he and the others referred to it. His travels had been made unusually quick with the aide of this trusty steed.

Not paying anymore attention to these events, Smitty returned to his chores of repairing the rims. He had over six that needed repair today alone. It was this backlog that had caused him to arise so early this morning. Although he personally liked the boy, he could not devote any more of his time today to his troubles. Secondly, Smitty knew that deep down inside this child was a bad sort and to retain the contract that he had strive for so long he would eventually have to distance himself from him. Smitty's thoughts wandered and reflected on these early morning events. *Would Thomas, if he had survived, turn out this way? Would these two young men have been friends?*

Smiling to himself, Smitty continued his work and watched the hot metal take the desired shape in front of him between anvil and hammer, oblivious to the fact that even now he was being watched from a dark corner across the street, as Tristan made his escape.

"Where have you been? Mum's been asking for you."

Turning his attention rather casually, the young boy reached up grabbed the bridle to control the animal and remarked "Nice horse, where did you get him?"

Then, just as quickly, he turned back to the main conversation. "Did you get the money?" asked Henry.

Henry looked up to Tristan as all of the others did. Most of the time when Mona, or Mum, to the boys was not around they all looked to Tristan or "The Duke", as he was known; for most of the residents of the "hole" considered Tristan as "The Archduke of the Wharf".

Ever since his father was placed in debtor's prison when Tristan was a wee lad, Tristan had to make his own way in the streets. Learning his *craft* through people like Mona, Tristan had become a master at the art of deception and thievery. The decrepit basement of an abandon building was their home. Dark, damp and musty rodents scurried about and the smell of human feces filled the air. The basement, at one time, served as a coal tunnel to bring coal directly from the docks. The coal was then provided the building above with heat. The building, now long since dilapidated, was the former inner-city monastery long since condemned with the fall of Catholicism. This was Mona's *kingdom.* Here she ruled the collection of homeless children with an iron fist, and Tristan was the *Crown Prince.* As such "The Duke was free to set his own course and to train the others in the *Craft.*

"How's the old girl doing", responded Tristan. Blasted fever, first took his own mother when he was but four, then with her passing, it was too much for his own Pa. That's what drove him to drink, Tristan reminded himself. If it weren't for the fever, his Ma and Pa would still be around to take care of him and teach him a thing or two. The only connection that Tristan had retained of this past life, through all of this destitution and misery was his father's gold locket and chain which he, as his father had, wore around his neck. Inside this tiny locket was a lock of his mother's hair. The hair inside used to have a sweet smell to it, almost like flowers, Tristan recalled, but time and the living conditions of the *hole* had changed that.

Clutching the locket tightly as he often did, Tristan wondered, *how many times had he fallen asleep holding this very locket?* He had sought comfort in holding this locket for years; it had *become* his mother for his memory of her had faded. All he remembered was her smell, the same that the hair once held. What a beautiful smell that was, not like here. He often felt that if heaven ever had a scent, it would be her. His father once told him that his mother would read to him and rock him to sleep. Someday… his mind wondered in endless thought… he might even learn to read. Maybe, just maybe he could find someway to take care of this fever problem so that others would not have to suffer his own fate; but not here, not now. Over the years he had grown accustom to periodically touching his chest to not only remind himself of the past but to also to provide reassurance that the locket was still there. Sometimes onlookers thought that Tristan had a bad heart, which gave him an advantage in some cases and pity in others.

"She ain't good", remarked Henry. "We gots to 'elp her The Duke! She can't pass; we ain't got no one else! You ain't good neither" remarked the lad as he watched Tristan go through the ritual of feeling the locket.

Tristan looked down at the dirty little face in front of him. Henry was about seven or maybe eight-ish. As Tristan stood there with Henry's little face cupped in his hands he drifted in thought once again. Faces change, conditions don't. How many children had Tristan seen pass through here? How many times would he train someone only to have them arrested, or worse, take ill and pass on as his mother had? How could it have come to this? If there was a God… why? What had this little filthy excuse for a human being done, or anyone else down here for that matter to deserve such a life? Why continue to allow such an existence to go on? These thoughts danced in his head as he stood there in front of the child, as water dripped down from the streets and structures above.

"On't worry came the delayed response. "With 'nough quid, anything is possible"

"But where do we get such, The Duke" asked Henry.

"I know just the place, the customhouse, it will soon be loaded and ripe for the pinch" came the response. Tristan had long watched the crates offloaded from numerous swift men-of-war that rotated in and out of the harbor. It was not until recently he had learned of their holdings. These fast small ships were rumored to be of Francis Drake the gallant English lord who preyed on the Spanish fleet coming from far away…some place called New Spain. *I never knew there was an old one let alone a new one,* Tristan mused.

From the stories on the street Drake was revered more than the Queen especially by Tristan and his followers. Drake, the swashbuckling Prince of the Sea! Oh, to serve him, what a dream! If the latest rumors were to be believed, Drake was sailing around the world plundering the Spanish fleet in his wake!

"When I was checking out the house last night I got into a wee spot. Had to spend the night on the wharf I did. I overheard from the guards that another ship is due in late by weeks end. I'm glad to see that you made it back okay."

Tristan was referring to the fact that Henry had gone to the wharf with him but had his own *mission* to accomplish. "Did you check out the ship's schedule like I asked" Tristan inquired of the boy before him.

Continuing in his questioning, Tristan asked, "Do you know when the ship is coming in?"

"Aye" came the response, "what ever is on board", continued Henry in a semi-state of excitement, "took 'um four days to load and is to be stored in Customs 'til first light."

"Great!" exclaimed Tristan, "but when are they due in?"

"Me source say that they are due in five days hence. Drake himself is comin! After three years at sea he's due at Plymouth, the rest is comin 'ere." Almost shouting the younger boy was now jumping up and down.

"Okay, okay, is it comin with the tide?"

"Aye, with the tide", came the response.

"Great!" exclaimed Tristan again, "that gives us the darkness…we hit then!"

"But The Duke, what of the guards?"

"Let me worry 'bout them", Tristan replied. "Here, take this" he said to Henry. Tristan handed the boy a small leather bag that contained a small sum of coins. "Get this to the Apothecary for the syrup…and be quick about it! Now I need to be with Mona."

Departing the younger child and heading down the dark passageway, Tristan could see that at least five of the others had gathered on the brick shelf above. Turning to look over his shoulder, Tristan could see that Henry was still standing there looking after him longingly. To help redirect the younger boy's mind, Tristan rather cavalierly said as he walked into the darkness that was their home, "and have someone take back me steed to Smitty!"

Mona did not look good. Her fever was raging and was taking its toll. Her skin had that grayish clammy appearance which indicated to Tristan that her time on this earth was short. Not able to eat for several days she was weakened to the state that she was almost delusional. Tristan knew that if she did not receive help soon it would render all other assistance useless. He wondered if this was what it was like for his own mother in her final days. "*What went through me Pa's mind? Was it similar to those thoughts that I now share?*" Approaching carefully as to not disturb her, Tristan just wanted to be close to her. Most would have considered her to be an ugly woman, wretched in thought and deed. Her hair was mostly gone due to lice and she bore the scares of an earlier bought with the pox. She was filthy and her clothes raggedy just like the children that she controlled. But to Tristan as well as nearly 10 other homeless children, she was "Mum". Tristan and the others had accepted this woman when others on the streets above would not. She took care of them when they too had been sick and provided them with leadership as well as advice. It was disturbing that now that she needed similar assistance, the boys were helpless without the funds necessary to purchase or otherwise obtain the medicines for her. She had taught them to steal, and did this well. But the medicines had to be mixed just right by an educated person in order to help her. This was not something they could steal. As he drew closer, he could hear her coughing. It was a low crouping cough from deep within her. As she coughed she spit up yellow mucus into a bowl next to her. The bowl was now filled almost to the top with similar spitals.

"The Duke, is that you," she choked out as he approached.

"Yes Mum, it is me, I'm here for you."

"Bless you child, you are such a good lad not to forget your old Mum. Did you get the quid?"

"Aye, Mum I got it" Tristan was rather reluctant to tell her the truth.

She was expecting him to have already obtained some of the holdings from the Customs House. Tristan did not have the heart to tell her that it would not be in port until later in the week. But for now he had some money that he hoped would buy enough medicine to hold her over. However, from her appearance, he did not believe that she would make it until the end of the week. So what ever he told her now, he was already convinced that he would be accountable only in the afterlife. She coughed violently now and again spit up more sputum, this time it was laced with blood clots. *"This is not good."* He thought as he reached out and held her hand.

"I've already sent out for the meds…you hold on now… it will be okay," he said. Patting her head with a cool wet towel that lay nearby he lifted her head slightly. Supporting her shabby head with one hand he picked up the small water bowl next to her and gave her a sip of water.

Meanwhile, in another part of the country yet another play in this tale was busy pursuing his dream, not knowing what the future truly held for him.

"Don't wait up tonight, my dear. The elders are to render their opinion of my proposal."

In the village of Auld, the church elders were as powerful as the Queen. The elders controlled everything and everyone. To get approval for a new shop, marriage, birth or what ever it was, the formal request had to go before the elders. But, then again, as John reminded himself, *that's why he lived here.* He had longed dreamed of a church regulated world and Auld was as close as he would find in England.

"Is that the one where you wish to involve the criminals and insane into the parish" his wife asked?

"Please, I've asked you numerous times not to refer to them in that manner. We are all children of our Lord and these wretched souls need tending as well as our own."

"Well for your sake, I trust they will make the right decision, certainly you are incapable", his wife replied.

Ever since his father converted the family from Catholicism to the Church of England, John had a passion to spread the word of the Lord to all that would listen. No one had ever seen a more devote; yet strict and loving believer in the Word than John. His marriage, arranged as it was in those times amongst the well to do, had turned out all right, even though his wife, Isabel, was almost fifteen years his younger and with that, quite outspoken. *Youth!* John thought the problem with youth is that it is wasted on the young. If only his Christian convictions had been as strong then as they are now, what wonders he could have done for the Lord!

"I won't wait up for you", replied Isabel, as she combed her waist length golden blonde hair.

As John looked on, he wondered what color that truly was. God surely moves in wondrous ways. How could He take a rib and create such a beautiful creature as this? That was truly a miracle. Her hair was a golden yellow with a hint of brown, similar to that of the fabled Palomino on the continent, but yet the texture was softer than any rose petal John had ever felt.

That combined with the rose water Isabel used, made her a vision that was only worthy of heaven. And her scent, oh what a lovely scent that was! *What a pity,* John thought to him self with deep reflection, *that the Church had outlawed this practice of ancient Rome for so many years. But how does a little scent do harm?*

Purely distinctive of Isabel, John could smell her before he could see her. The aroma would last for hours it seemed long after she had left the room or put down the towel or other object that she was handling. He had made a mistake once and referred to this wonderful aroma differently. It was not received very well, funny how just one little word can give a whole new meaning to a phrase for some people. He chuckled to himself, although it was scarcely audible, as he reminded himself of her comment to his suggestion that her aroma was a smell. She had told him quite emphatically that swine had a smell, she did not! It didn't matter; to John it was the loveliest and yet intriguing scent that he had ever encountered. It was ambrosia and could make even the purest man go insane. *It must be hereditary,* John thought, *although I don't remember her mother with such a scent? Funny,* chuckling again to himself, *I wonder if it came from her father.* He shuttered at this idea and quickly put that out of his mind. It was funny, however. This scent has to be hereditary, for John felt from time to time that he could detect it on his own daughter. Some day he knew that she too would drive the young men wild. This would be of no fault of her own for his daughter was an upstanding young lady in all respect. But she shared her mother's curse of beauty and charm. With the addition of this wonderful scent, the young lads of Auld would be rendered helpless. This, of course, would be beneficial in finding her a successful husband, but would also work to her detriment in such a small and religious setting as Auld. Therefore John was dedicated to ensuring that his child received a quality life. This meant that she would have to marry a successful gentleman, possibly from London. In order to succeed in this pursuit, she would first have to receive a quality education. That was not going to happen in Auld!

Nonetheless, John felt that of all the wonders he had experienced, Isabel was the most stunning. And yet he remained distant from her. To tell her exactly what she meant to him or how he felt for her would be considered blasphemous. John's dogmatic view of a Christian life and his rather stuffy upbringing often hampered his ability to pass on compliments. To be overtly intimate with someone was truly out of the question! To extend matters, John was older than her and felt unworthy of her affection. He was old and seemed to be getting older by the moment. His skin had started to wrinkle and hang in loose pockets. He was considered to be a large man and not overly handsome. As a matter of fact, in the polite circles of London John had been considered rather homely. It was always the talk of such circles of how he ever managed to wed such a wonderful prize as Isabel. The sequel to this, of course was how such a wonderful *catch* as Isabel stayed married to him. Of course there was always speculation of such things and on more than one occasion, John overheard them. It was in these times that John's self confidence, which was outwardly considered to be extensive, but inwardly was quite shallow, would be shaken.

Most people considered him to be a very confident and capable person, but the secret that John held inside was that this outward appearance was merely a facade. His responses to such "slips of the tongue" were generally met with a fierce anger, normally directed at the unsuspecting Isabel. This, in turn, just added to his suspicions that someday she would find a way to be rid of him.

As a large man John generally had trouble in moving around, which gave him an almost lumbering appearance. In his advanced years his pains from his earlier days in the mines trying to learn his father's trade from the inside, as his father had insisted, came back to haunt him. This was especially true on the cooler mornings. Most recently his body seemed destine to further distance itself from all others by adapting the condition of flatulence, and if that were not enough… impotence. All of this added to his supposition that the only form of affection such a beautiful creature could ever bestow upon him would be out of pity not love, which infuriated John even more. He would not be pitied by anyone!

John's distance from Isabel had complicated their marriage to the extent that they only had the one child, now coming of age at thirteen. Her name was rather an unusual one for this northern England village, but none the less, Isabel adorned the name, and so it stuck; Thomasin Lynn. Thomasin, except for age, was the twin of Isabel. She had the same golden/yellow/brown hair, skin softer than any goose down or rose petal and big bright green eyes. Smarter than any other child in the one room school house of Auld, Isabel was heartbroken when John felt it best to send the young girl off to receive a "Christian education". This was particularly difficult for both mother and child. But John knew that for her to have a better life, it was necessary. However, with the transformation of the Kingdom to Protestant, it brought on the demise of the age-old practice of sending young girls to the Convent.

By using his family name for an advantage, John secured a place for his daughter in a Christian school in the Calais area of Northern France. This area was still marked by heavy English influence, although it was lost to the English monarch some thirty years previous. John felt that his daughter may have a better chance at assimilating in this particular area, but he could have never had been more wrong. The last thing that the locals wanted was yet another rich English person at their doors, rich perceived or not! The decision was particularly hard on Thomasin for she did not speak French nor did she have the desire to learn French or their customs.

Thomasin had been gone now for almost eight months and from her absence, Isabel grew lonely. As long as Thomasin was around, Isabel had a friend. They had been constant companions and shared the most intimate of secrets. Not a typical mother-daughter relation at all especially in rural England, but one that little girls everywhere often only dream of.

From her parent's relationship and discussions thereof, which did her mother share; Thomasin questioned her father's love. She saw and witnessed first hand the pain inflicted on Isabel by her father's demeanor and distance from his wife. Both Isabel and Thomasin grew to question the concept of *Christian love* and resentful of the time that John spent with others in order to further *God's work*. Often Isabel would confide in Thomasin that John's distance was taken as rejection. Further, Isabel would warn Thomasin of the *trap of love* for Isabel was only 12 when she married, which aided in the closeness between the two.

John, on the other hand, believed that his wife had lost what little respect she held for him and her attitude now bordered on despising him. His large bulky frame and penchants for anger only added to her arrogance. Things had not been the same between them since Thomasin was born. Shortly after their child's birth, John's father died; leaving John in line to inherit a substantial sum of money and holdings, including the family's coalmines located just outside of London. These coalmines would have made John and Isabel, easily some of the richest in London, save the Queen of course.

But this is when the problems began.

"It is easier for a camel to pass through the eye of a needle than for a rich man to go to heaven"; John was often heard quoting.

Ever since he spent that summer with the Archbishop of Canterbury, John had renewed his devotion to religion and now believed he had found Gods work. When he passed his inheritance to his younger brother and picked up the mantle of Christianity, Isabel felt betrayed. And so, they moved new baby and all, to this small farm village in the northern country to begin a church.

Far removed from this English setting across the ocean to the *New World* was yet another pivotal player in the events that were to transpire.

Sipping at the cool drink customary for this time of the day, Señor Juan Diego Hectorgaudo del Vargas, or Hector to his acquaintances pushed away the sheer curtain meant for protection from the local insects; especially those nasty mosquitoes and the sickening disease they brought. As he strolled out on to the veranda he twirled the stem of the glass of light fruit drink between two fingers. He contemplated what marvelous fortune that had just been bestowed upon him. *Wouldn't his family back in Spain be amazed* he thought. Born the son of a stable hand and running away from home at the age of twelve, no one could have imagined that he would have survived on his own let alone prospered as he did. Joining the army and moving through the lower ranks seemed to be as natural as breathing to Hector. Volunteering for the "Expedition" that most felt was fool-hearty actually became a blessing in disguise. Serving with honor and distinction on the battlefield as well as on the more personal side for his commander Cortéz, Hector won that which was most uncommon for his day, the right to rise to Officer-ship and the "landed gentry". Serving both Cortéz and the Governor de León, Hector received not only land grants but also a full military commission from the Crown. This propelled Hector to the right of title, something that would have been impossible for anyone with a family such as his if he has stayed in Spain. But this was New Spain, a place for a new beginning, even though the new Governor was reportedly different than de León, Hector reassured himself that he too could turn in time.

His tall, lanky frame and jet-black wavy hair presented an image that was actually quite striking, although somewhat unusual for this area. His black hair adorned feathery white skin that appeared to be almost translucent at times. Long slender fingers with sharp pointed nails did not aid in his appearance. Fellow soldiers often felt that by appearance alone this gave him a somewhat feminine quality. This, of course, only added to the rumors of how quickly he had risen in rank.

Hector's ego had swelled over the years to the point now, with this newest assignment, he was actually quite unbearable, even to the local villagers. Fancying himself as the ladies man, Hector was well known amongst the locals. Here, he found the local women with attributes different from home and an air of submission that enticed him. One that he had been particularly fond of had the audacity to become pregnant! If that was not enough, the witch claimed the bastard as his! When she complained to the local officials, however, that was too much. Now he had to take care of her, the leech. The child did, however, have some similarities that even Hector had to admit. She was tall, thin, very light skin and had wavy hair. Not like the locals at all. Thus, by official decree, she became *his* anyway. No matter he thought, and gave them quarter and employment at the edge of his hacienda. From time to time when he grew tied of the local stock, he still granted them favors, sometimes both at the same time. *"Ah, Life is good",* thought Hector as he smiled.

His appointment as the Supreme Military Commander; charged with the protection of His Majesty's gold shipments in the Caribbean and New Spain was his latest achievement.

A position that he had created was certainly destine for glory. Glory which of course he could use to his own benefit and curry women's favor when he moved back home. With a smile, Hector thought of how he would move back home, transferring his title and holdings to a large estate in the country. He of course would employ his family as servants. That should bring justice! Hector believed himself to have had a poor childhood with repressive and cruel parents. Running away as he did at the age of twelve was to seek relief.

This new assignment was going to be rather boring however. Not like the adventures with de León or Cortéz. He would have plenty of time on his hands, time enough to continue the plot and plow the field of the locals, naturally. He would have to be careful though, he had heard of a new illness. This way was certainly the work of the Devil; some even said they were related. This illness caused painful sores in the genitals, a rash and painful urination! *"Not good"*…he thought and gave a shutter.

Boring yes, but time. Boring because aside for the prospect of an occasional native uprising or maybe bandits along the coast, there was no threat, no challenge no one literally, to protect the shipments from, except *him* and the occasional English bandit. Considering he had the receipts and the bill of laden, who would know if he shaved some off?

Shaved off… he thought! What another terrific idea of his! After all he should be "compensated" for his idea to produce bars anyway. In his former position as the head of gold production, Hector made the suggestion that rather than sending gold nugget or artifacts back to Spain, which *was too easy to log and record*, he thought; packaging, shipping, and handling would be more efficient if the gold was smelted down into rectangular shapes. Soon he would have to transfer his skills over to the mining of silver, which was quickly out pacing that of gold. The local officials bought off on the idea and when the Court realized that more gold could be shipped in this manner, they too were all for it. What a wonderful ruse! The natural extension of this of course was some "loyal" subject would be relied upon to produce the engineering design. That task fell to Hector.

The design he came up with was forty-five centimeters long, sixteen centimeters wide weighing in at forty kilograms. If 1 centimeter was shaved off all the way around this bar, the net gain would be a little over three kilograms per bar. (one should not be too greedy) However and here was the best, it was Hector who would file the report and drawings to the territory officials! So he simply filed the report that the gold bars would be shipped at a finished dimension of forty-four centimeters by fifteen centimeters. What a plan! Hector laughed now outwardly at the overt stupidity of others. Now he knew, of course that he could not just come up with gold shavings such as this, so the shavings were transported in secret back to his village, and reprocessed into local trinkets. When the time was right, he would use it to frame some Spanish official that he did not like and turn the whole lot into the King. Then as a reward, Hector would establish his own land and title in Spain and leave this Godforsaken place all behind, *along with the witch that tried to ruin him with a child*, again he laughed, this time so hard he nearly choked.

Her name was Mariá. Her mother had given her a Spanish name hoping that she would be accepted. It didn't work. Outcaste by the Spanish, particularly her father, the Señor del Vargas, Mariá was not accepted by her mother's people either. Although the Spanish viewed her as a native, her mother's people saw her as Spanish. She did bear the resemblance of her father. Tall, thin, very light skin, although tan, or rather the color of coffee or the little nut that the Spanish loved. *Oh, what did they call those things;* she pondered raising a finger to her lips as she concentrated on the thought. *Oh, yes…I remember oliva…*or olives!

Mariá lived, for the most part, with her mother just outside del Vargas' home. *What a magnificent home it was,* Mariá thought. *Why it was large enough for all the villagers to have their own space with room left over for the animals!*

As she stood on the dusty road that led back to her village and at the base of the hacienda's tall mud stone outer walls she recalled the stories of its construction. One evening, while sitting around the council fire, the elders relayed the story of its construction to her, for it was built long before Mariá was even thought of. The home was built originally for the territorial governor. Tiles and roofing material had been brought over from the temples of the Aztecs. Craftsmen and artists from the ancient capital city were also brought in to supervise the locals in the construction project. It was during this construction that the first of several failed revolts occurred. It was explained that there was a very old man that had refused to bow when the Señor, then a very young man, rode by. As was the custom imposed in those days, all villagers were to bow and remove any headdress that they may have whenever the visitors passed. This particular man, a very proud man and at one time considered to be one of the better and more accomplished warriors, refused. The Señor ran him through with his sword. Then, if this was not enough, rumors tell the story of how the Señor ordered the others to cut up the old man and mix his pieces into the mud bricks. This story, whether true or not, recorded events many years ago and gave almost a mystical or ominous air to the home. The hacienda sat atop of a high ridgeline that took a commanding view of the village and actually the entire island, prefect for defending. On the backside, where the sleeping quarters were, was a small tropical garden perched on the edge of a sharp cliff. At the base of this cliff lied the ocean whose powerful waves created a sound that lulled the visitors to sleep every night. Legends speak of the night winds of early autumn drawing out the cries of the laborers that built this home and most notably the old man who was now a part of it. On certain nights, wailing could still be heard through the walls as the winds passed through.

On most days she kept her mother company, helping her gather fruits and nuts or tilling the soil. That was particularly important now because as her mother grew older, the man who once sought her favor did not come to her bed as much any more. Nor did he provide them with the stipend that he was supposed to by official ruling. So now in her older age Mariá's mother had to scrape by the best she could. How could Mariá tell her mother that Señor del Vargas now visited her own bed rather than her mothers? The thought of him coming around almost every night sickened her! This was supposed to be her father, did he know this? What's this God of the visitors that would allow such a thing, Mariá questioned. As Mariá grew older her long, jet-black hair started to turn wavy, just like the Señor. It repulsed her even more.

Sometimes to escape this despair Mariá would take up the company of another outcast from local society. This was an older woman that lived by herself on the other side of the island. She was considered to be a *Civatateo* priest by the local people. Although Mariá lived far from the main center of the Aztec Empire, the influence of these rich and at one time powerful people reached far throughout the region. The natives believed that the old woman was once a noblewoman who had died during childbirth and had since returned to earth, thus earning her the title of this creature. In actuality she was not, but the follower of a much more sinister sort. For she was an accomplished priest of *Malinalxochi;* who was believed to be a sorceress with special powers over the stinging insects of the world. It was through these insects, most notably the scorpion, that the old woman claimed her fame. As such she was endowed with magical powers. This priest, or as the Spanish referred to her, *bruja* or witch, was one who spoke to the village gods which were the same gods as the legendary Aztecs. The Spanish were particularly fearful of her.

Ignorant of her ways and power, the Spanish banished her to the other side of the island. Priests were looked upon to be the foundation of culture and religion amongst the native peoples. These natives at one time easily outnumbered the Spanish and if they could consolidate under one leader, even now in their depleted numbers could easily overrun the meager garrison. In order to prevent this, the Spanish felt it necessary to divide the people and dissolve this local culture. By doing so they were also able to introduce Christianity to the local population and thus validate their presence. They banned the use of the native tongue and religion. This was a good thing to the Europeans for it also meant the dissolution of human sacrifices. To keep the population divided and leaderless the old woman was removed to the other side of the island. The natives however, would often visit her, and bring her subsistence. In return she would treat their ills or take revenge on their enemies. More than one Spaniard had "mysteriously" met their fate while they slept! It was rumored that even del Vargas had been a target of the curse of *Tezcatlipoca*. This was the Aztec god of the night who was said to possess a magic mirror that would give off a toxic smoke and kill those that he was sent to visit. On two separate occasions a loyal servant broke the curse, however before it could take its desired affect. In their beliefs of *Tezcatlipoca*, if the curse is broken by the hand of a true believer on three separate occasions, the priest that sent him would meet their eternal doom and die a thousand deaths.

Most people found the old woman to be revolting. She was shriveled and was stark white in appearance, as if she were already dead. She had a crackling sound to her voice and always spoke in rather short verses or parables. She did possess powers however, that mortals found difficult to understand. However, Mariá found comfort in her and became a very willing student of the old ways. *Besides*, Mariá thought to herself, *this also provided refuge from the nightly visits by her father…revolting!* Mariá shuttered at the passing thought.

In time Mariá became the trusted associate of the priest often confiding in her as a daughter to a mother. Always eager to help her surrogate mother, one afternoon shortly before sunset Mariá was helping her gather moist herbs and a few insects required for the treatment of a horrible skin rash one of the natives had developed. In their time alone on the hillside over looking the lagoon not far from where she lived, Mariá asked the question that had been burning inside her since they first met.

Turning to the older woman, Mariá asked inquisitively, "how did you learn your trade? I mean I've heard the stories of the villagers but I find them rather hard to believe. So, if I assume these stories are not true, then how did you gain such marvelous powers over the ordinary things of the earth?"

Quietly placing her reed basket down on the plush tropical floor, the old woman's demeanor suddenly changed. She no longer had the look of a forest hag, but one of a tired, yet still passionate woman, who just felt the weight of a thousand years of misunderstandings and insults lifted from her bosom. Smiling at Mariá, the look was obviously unpracticed and hideous, rather frightful, but yet for the first time since they met nearly two years hence, Mariá found a human in the figure before her.

"My dear child" she began with her infamous crackling voice which started to soften, "I, like I'm sure you, had dreams as a child. I dreamed of a man and children. I dreamed of a home to call my own. But this was not my calling, for the gods had different plans."

She looked around and soon found a comfortable spot to sit. Once doing so she motioned for Mariá to join her. As soon as she did, the old woman continued. "My dear, I am not originally from the Aztecs you see. My people were from a more ancient culture than they. I come from the ancient red city of *Tulum*. This was a grand city, full of food and bright shiny cloth. Most of the other peoples would come and offer gifts to our gods… it was a grand time and a beautiful place to be a child. It over looked the sea, up on a high bluff and the winds always brought the cool air."

She paused in reflectance closing her water-filled eyes as if to draw in the sense of memory until it was complete.

A moment passed as Mariá and the old woman sat in quiet reflectance. Then, the old woman gave Mariá a gentle pat and continued her tale. "You see when what remained of our city fell to the Aztecs; I was to be a virgin sacrifice to the war god *Huitzilopochtli*. My father was a great warrior but was held as disgraced in battle by the city's fall. As such as a measure of atonement I was sent to the capital as a virgin sacrifice. I remember the day as if it were yesterday." The old woman once again gave pause to reflect. "To further my father's shame, my mother started to cry uncontrollably and ran after me. She ran after her only child through the dusty side streets of my home village. To re-establish his pride and himself as the center of his house, my father caught up with her and cut her down just as she was reaching out to me."

With this remembrance, tears started to flow, even after all these years and it made Mariá feel guilty for asking the question.

But the old woman continued, "I was taken across country to the capital. Here I was stripped and bathed in oils and flowers, fitting for the sacrifice. Incense was burned and the priest entered the room chanting to the great god. The priest was there to administer the last of the rites and to offer the herbs that would take my thoughts to the underworld and dull my external pain. This was necessary" the old woman explained, "because screaming was sacrilegious and bode evil upon the sacrifice. It was at this moment that the gods showed I was for another purpose. For as the head priest walked forward, the last of the foam from the bathing oils flowed away revealing my mark."

With this the old woman paused as if to collect her breath and her emotions for this recollection was visibly painful to her.

Stammering at the story, Mariá interjected, "mark? What mark do you speak?"

"The mark that I was born with, the mark on my bosom. It is this mark that had kept me a virgin for as long as it had." Then smiling again she said as almost a side note, "I did have other offers! The mark is that of a scorpion, or at least that is what is seen. Well, when the head priest saw this mark, he decided that to serve the gods better, I should be *attached* to the temple and be learned in the ways of *Malinalxochi* the sorceress.

In time I grew in my understanding and soon became an accomplished priest. The world was mine to control.

Even Montezuma himself would call upon me for advice and assistance in battle. When the visitors arrived, it was I who had incorrectly advised that their leader was the Feathered-Snake god, *Quetzalcoatl* who had promised to return. For my failure, I banished myself to this place. And now the visitors come even here! But it is this life that I brought to my people and caused our great nation to fall like a feather in the wind so many moons ago. And it is from this life that the locals, your mother's people, know me by. I do what I can for them, but they have to be strong to maintain their own culture. They cannot confront the Spanish by means of weaponry these days are long past. Their fire-sticks are too powerful. Maybe my child it is you who can teach them another way."

"Me?" questioned Mariá, raising a finger to her chest and with a look of astonishment.

"Yes, I think you my child. For it is said that one of mixed blood shall rise and relieve the suffering of these simple people, one with a tender and unspoiled heart. You are the first to ask of my past as if I was truly human. And from your question, I become human once more."

The rest of the afternoon passed in silence as Mariá pondered the words of the priest.

Visiting the priest more and more frequent as she developed into young womanhood, Mariá started to take over some of her trade. The words of the priest reverberated in her soul and made Mariá determined to become what she now believed was her destiny. Soon Mariá's fame spread throughout the territory. Although the Spanish had outlawed the art of human sacrifice and forced Christianity on the locals, the old ways did not dissipate as easily. Providing little more than just the motions of loyal servants of the singular god the villagers started to resurrect the religions and gods of the past, with Mariá's help, of course. Most of their ceremonies were held at night, near the lagoon of the priest. Village warriors were sent out to pray on other island peoples to bring in sacrifices to the re-established gods. Pride was returning to the people and with pride an ease of the suffering seemed imminent. Had *Quetzalcoatl* finally favored them? With all the disease, death and misery that the people had endured was the patron god of the Aztecs, the "feathered- snake and creator sky-god coming to save them? These and many other rumors of Mariá abound to the point where del Vargas hearing the claims felt it necessary to dispel them. This he figured was necessary to maintain control over the local population and not give rise to some fantasy that would entice the locals to revolt.

The rumors took on new meaning when the Spaniards went out against her and were turned back by a strange, yet powerful storm that seemed to arise from no where and end just as sudden. The villagers claimed that she called upon *Tlaloc* the god of rain to defend her, where in actuality it was just a tropical storm most common to the area.

When the old woman past on, most felt it was Mariá. It was rumored that Mariá, eager to gain control had stolen her spirit, which only added to her own stigma. But this stigma served her well. Now del Vargas was no longer interested in her or for her shapely body, for he had found another. *Or perhaps he was fearful himself of what she might be able to do*, Mariá often wondered. Nonetheless, Mariá now curried his favor and was allowed to live inside the hacienda walls of the Señor. She became a… *"Oh what did he call her?"* Mariá paused… *"usted es mi pagador de fortuna"* or my fortune-teller. *"What a laugh, I can't tell someone's fortune, only the future"*, Mariá found humor in the Spanish ignorance of such things.

As Mariá pondered such things, back across the waters, John was in pursuit of his goal.

"But Brother Viccars, can you explain to me and the rest of these good people why exactly we should consider your proposal" asked the chief elder of the Anglican order.

"Elder Wilson", John replied, "it is a travesty the way the insane and the criminals are treated in our country." Standing before the counsel of elders John finally had the stage to plead his case. Standing before them John rested his mighty hands upon the table in front of him. "For England to assume its rightful place as leader of the world, we, as a civilized society must ensure that all of our citizens are treated fairly, we need to protect their rights and educate them in the Christian form of living. How can we call ourselves Christians yet treat these people in such draconian manner? Chaining the insane to a wall and beating them until they are unconscious is not what I consider the Christian thing to do. Most of these poor wretched souls are suffering from malnutrition, scurvy, lice and leprosy. How can we as a modern society continue to look the other way? As for the criminal, most of those so-called criminals are in prison because they could not pay debts or they had a different view than our leaders. How does this condition constitute any resemblance to civilization; when we allow a prison to be formed of bread, swill, rats and disease?"

"I'm moving on this now…they're listening…it won't be long 'till they see this my way, I'm sure of it," John thought to himself as he spoke.

"If they could not pay their debts before they went to prison, how are they to do it after they come out?" he reasoned. "My proposal would bring these souls here to Auld from around the shire, at first, then if successful, from the remainder of the kingdom. Here in Auld we can treat them along Christian values, nurse them to health and when they are rehabilitated, return them to society so they may once again be a productive member."

The chief elder just sat there for a moment. Silence filled the air like a heavy fog. Elder Wilson was a clutching, grasping sort of man. One who looked perpetually old. He possessed that sort of look as if to say, if you came back in a hundred years he would still be here and just as old. If he was not such a devote Christian, most certainly he would be in politics. Certainly not some one you would buy a horse from! Elder Wilson controlled almost everything and everyone in Auld. He owned the majority of the township and was also serving as the chief constable. His personal hygiene was noteworthy, but not in the good sense. He had an existing odor of rotten meat in his scraggly white beard, which was all of about five hairs, and in which one could always find remains of his last meal. His yellow teeth, certainly not his own, were reportedly from a dead man, which was quite common in these days of advanced dentistry. The thought caused John to shutter. He would much rather have the older fashion wood teeth than that of a dead man's in his mouth.

Then Elder Wilson began to speak. His raspy, airy voice was almost like geese squawking. "I do not see how this would benefit the good people of this shire to bring the criminals and insane to our doors. I believe that your Christian intents are honest but ill advised. Your remarks with regards to the official policies of this land are borderline sedition. I would watch myself if I were you young man", said the elder as he pointed his long slender finger at John. "Your words may be met at the end of a rope. You should tend to that young wife of yours and leave such matters as these to others. Such a pretty little thing should not be left at home on nights such as this". His words were edged on filthy intent John thought and even though he was a man of the *cloth* so-to-speak, Elder Wilson had an unspeakable character. Rumors only spoken to the discrete from behind closed doors revealed the darker side to his character. "A buggier of boys and young girls, even in his advanced age were often said of him.

Truly not a man to take such words of filthy intent lightly, Elder Wilson despised any idea other than his own. John knew, however, that his idea was just and true. He also knew that it was his only chance to have a flock of his own. His advanced age played against him. The senior father of the parish was a much younger man.

Realizing that without the support of Elder Wilson, his mission was doomed to failure before it even started. Rejected,

John walked home through the streets of Auld alone. He was often this way, he thought. Lacking a true friend or relation, loneliness had become almost a cloak to bear. So many times this had been the course he found paved for him. He knew that Christianity was the key for him, to quell his own inner anger. But somehow he had to separate himself from the past and establish himself in this world and away from his father. John, if nothing else, was his own person not the mere shadow of someone else. *"Was Christianity the method or merely the path? If only others really knew him,"* he thought, *"it would not be this way!"*

After meandering through the back streets for what seemed to be an eternity, John finally came to his door. He knew what lied on the other side. How could he face her, he thought. The creaking of the hinge announced his arrival.

"John, is that you?" Isabel was still awake!

"Yes", not wishing to carry the conversation any farther.

"Turned you down didn't they" Isabel remarked. A response typical from only a wife.

"Yes, my love, your wish came true" John replied.

"Serves you right. Thomasin and I should be dinning with London's finest now. But you have to turn rightist on me. First the mine now this. Where will it end? Here I am stuck in this little provincial town without even a proper garment shoppe. And poor Thomasin, whisked off to God knows where…"

John could not let her continue. He had had about all he could take from this shrew. If she knew of the monster that lurked within his soul, she would be more cautious. The only thing that John had ever found that could keep it in check was

Christianity. "Hush woman" replied John in a voice that was foreign to Isabel. "It is my choice; you have no place nor say. I would mind my tongue if I were you or you will find your self sleeping strapped to the whipping post." It was still customary to treat one's wife in this manner in this shire, John reminded her. Women who did not please or obey their husbands were frequently whipped publicly in Sherburne Shire. Just one of the many *advantages* of living here John thought to himself. He was in no mood for further conversation, just food and rest. "Did you prepare supper woman?"

"I did, for me, do you think you deserve something to eat" she quipped.

Not an untypical remark, he really did want any of her swill anyway. John opened the door and stepped back into the night slamming it shut behind him. The night was good; it was damp and dark perfect for hiding his rejection. Isabel could sleep alone tonight he thought; she certainly was no comfort to him or worthy of his company.

CHAPTER TWO

...Treasure and Friendship

The warm tropical sun glistened on the now tanned backs of the sailors as they labored with the heavy oak hatchway. The huge brass locks sealed the main cargo hold which was tightly shut. In his quarters off the poop deck the Little Captain-General, as his men referred to him was already planning his next move. They had held this position for several days now and it was just a matter of time before the enemy would arrive. Pondering over the stolen maps of this *Spanish Lake* he struggled with the translation. They did not seem to fit his calculations on the sextant. Out on deck the hold of the massive ship was finally breached revealing her concealed stores of wealth. Those sailors present were taken back by the glimmer and opulence that lay before them.

"Blimy" remarked one of the astonished crewmembers. "Looks at all that! There's 'nough 'ere to buy the throne right out from under the Queen!"

"Let me see" exclaimed another as he pushed his ship mate aside.

Then just as his friend had done seconds previously the second crewmember was equally thunderstruck and sat back on his haunches.

"Blimey", is all he could muster.

First Mate Geoffrey Mortrude cried out, as he pushed his way the through the growing crowd of sailors, "alright you blokes, let's get a move on! She ain't goin' to jump out! Put your backs in to it then men!"

The capture of the treasure ship *Cacafuego* was anything short of miraculous. His ships, down to only one from the original five that had rounded the horn were considerably smaller than its Spanish counterpart. With only seventy men under his command, the capture of such a prize with over two hundred aboard was, for the Spanish, an embarrassment! How could such a small force, in a leaky little tub defeat a 600-ton man-of-war turned treasure vessel?

The *Cacafuego* was not an easy target. The ship had a keel length of eighty-one feet and boasted twenty 24-pounders, ten on each side. These massive cannons were set low in the hull to pound through that of any attacker. The ship also boasted ten additional 16-pounders on each side. These were set higher than the 24's and could easily rip the sail and rigging of any attacking ship with chain shot, or the infamous "incendiary shot"; which were spiked balls wrapped with tar soaked rope. The flaming ball would lodge itself into the wooden hull of an approaching ship and ignite it. On board there was normally up to 100 heavily armed soldiers as well. Seemingly impregnable, Spanish Galleons were not without fault. First, the command was split onboard between the sea captain and the soldiers. These meant priorities were not always in unison. Secondly they were slow, only moving at a rate between four to eight knots under a good wind. The ships were often severely overcrowded and the men malnourished. The sea captains had a habit of underfeeding their men only to sell the excess rations to colonists in the New World for a nice tidy little profit.

The *Pelican* was the sole survivor of his five-ship fleet that had set sail from England ostensibly on a trading expedition two years henceforth. Renamed the *Golden Hind* as he rounded the Straits of Magellan and into the previously undisturbed waters of New Spain, Drake raided Spanish settlements at will. However, although he and his men conducted numerous raids almost unabated, the plundering was remarkably restrained. Neither Spanish nor natives were harmed intentionally. Subsequently there were very few casualties and loss of life.

When the three-masted, squared rigged ship *Cacafuego* was first sighted on the horizon, it was already late in the day. A Galleon's main advantage was its gunnery. If this advantage could be thwarted, the subsequent fall of the vessel would be similar to that of plucking a ripe plum.

Striking at dusk and relying on superior speed, Drake proved the "Master Strategist". The technique employed was one of English design. This was the practice of "grappling and boarding". Firing his heavy guns to bring down the masts and sails, Drake was able to sail close enough to hook on with grappling hooks and board the vessel. With the sails and rigging cluttering the deck and a split command, chaos and confusion disoriented the defenders long enough for the smaller force to defeat them. Although facing overwhelming odds, Drake's daring move defeated the surprised Spanish in a matter of minutes. And the capture of the treasure ship yielded unimaginable wealth.

The sailors sat on the deck basking in delusions of grandeur brought on by the thought of the potential share they would receive of what laid before them. Amongst the rich treasure on board, they discovered eighty-tons of gold, twenty-six tons of silver, thirteen cases of silver coin, and cases filled with pearls. Each case weighed more than two men and was approximately three and half feet long, two feet wide and approximately two feet high. Each were sealed with the Royal Seal of King Philip II of Spain and bound with a large brass lock. Securing the survivors below decks, his men set forth on the difficult task of transferring the treasure to the *Golden Hind*, now seemingly appropriately named.

His men, for the past several days, had been occupied in the transfer of the treasure. Now nearing completion, Drakes' attention once again focused on the completion of his ultimate goal. Just then, interrupting his train of thought the First Mate knocked on his cabin door.

"Captain, sir, we 'ound something you's may want to see!"

"What is it Geoffrey?"

"Them Spanish are doing somethin' different to the gold and silver. There ain't no more stuff!"

Astonished at the word of this and not understanding the outcome, Drake jumped up from his desk and went to investigate. Arriving at the hold of the ship, Drake lean over the side to take a look. Through the shadows and the eerie glow of torch light all he could see was stacks and stacks of what appeared to be rectangular shaped bars which appeared to be made from gold and silver.

"Amazing" he uttered in astonishment. "Well, so much easier for us to steal" cried Drake! "Break out their rum stocks! It's time to celebrate! Looks like we've bagged a good piece!"

Returning to his quarters Drake drew his attention back to the ultimate goal. To be the first Englishman to complete Magellan's goal of global circumnavigation!

Blast, he thought, then muttering aloud, "the first man to ever actually accomplish the goal"; for Magellan was killed on some tiny island by local natives and never returned home.

But before he could set a course back out to sea, however, he had to make much needed repairs to his ship. He also had to answer the question as to what to do with the survivors of the now captured Galleon.

Drake called to his First Mate, "Geoffrey, report on the damages."

"Aye-aye, sir" came the response.

Within a few minutes First Mate Geoffrey Mortrude knocked again on his captain's door.

"Request permission to 'nter sir"

"Granted!"

Although not officially under the Queen's service, the men often acted as if they were… *"Possibly out of the pride that I have brought to them"*, mused Drake.

"What news of damages we have" asked Drake.

"Leaks are reported in the forward and aft holds. The mizzen is cracked. Powder stores down and we lost three cannon."

"What of the other stores", questioned Drake.

"Food is down, so is water, but there be rum to make up for that, it do", exclaimed Geoffrey.

Geoffrey had served with Drake longer than any other crew member, and had entered his service shortly after Drake had recovered from his earlier mishap with the Spanish. About ten years older than his master, he was a skilled seaman but poor on strategy and map-reading. Hunched over due to service at sea, Geoffrey now looked more like a large troll than a seaman. But loyal he was and that always went a long way for Drake.

Walking out of his quarters and on to the Poop deck, Drake leaned over and clutched the rail. Looking down to the deck below he issued the order.

"Okay bring over some of the heavier guns. We want at least ten if possible."

The heavier guns, the 24-pounders were a prize possession. These were especially crafted in the Spanish Dutch colonies and were made of brass, a much more durable metal at sea.

"Strip the Galleon of all food and water supplies that are fit, take what ever powder and shot we can hold, and make ready to get under way!"

"Aye-aye Captain" responded the First Mate smartly turning and sliding down the ladder from the poop deck.

Reaching the lower deck the First Mate turned back around and looked back up at the Captain. "What of the crew" he questioned?

"Ah, a good question lad" returned Drake. "Assemble the men, we'll ask them!"

Assembling the men took no time at all. Each, it appeared had already helped themselves to the plentiful stocks of wine and rum. Fruits from New Spain and salted meats were also not overlooked. As the seventy or so men gathered on deck, four escaped African slaves stood front and center. These four Drake had found in the Caribbean on one of the many islands he had visited. All four were a ferocious lot and had been, at least at one time, trained as warriors. All four were from the same general area in Africa but of different tribes. The men had made the voyage from Africa several years ago and were sold to work in the gold mines of New Spain. Escaping in the middle of the night when the guards were drunk after some particular Spanish holiday, they had made their way with the help from a stolen local village boat to a sparsely populated island in the Caribbean. Here they met and were befriended by Drake. They had a particular interest in the fate of the Spanish and moving to the front of the assembled symbolized their newly established form of comradeship. The four stood intently, clubs and sword in hand, awaiting word from the Captain-General.

Standing on the Poop deck with his hands on the railing Drake addressed the assembled crew. "Men, fellow seamen, today is a great day for our country and the world! For today we mark the end of the repression of Spanish rule and begin a new-world order. You men, men all, who stand before me now, reflect the best in English seamanship. I am proud to have the privilege to serve with you. We now embark, however, on yet another fateful mission. To be the first to circumnavigate the world since 1522 and Magellan! The way ahead shall not be an easy one. I'm sure all of you recall our trip around the horn. The winds that day were such as if the bowels of the earth had set all at liberty; as if all the clouds under heaven had been called together to lay their force upon that one place. I will not stand before you now and try to convince you that this will not reoccur, or that we will ever see our homes again. But what I will promise you is that you will have your courage tested and see adventure. From where we are positioned now, for survival, our best bet is to continue on with our journey, and if successful, we should arrive back home within a year. Are you with me?"

A rousing cheer came from the group of assembled men. And then one spoke, undistinguished from the assembled. "What of 'hem?" pointing to the captured Spanish survivors. "What's we to do with 'em?"

"Good question", responded Drake. "Gentlemen, we are a free and independent democracy, so I ask you, a vote as to what we should do." Pausing for a moment Drake continued, "Do we set them a drift as they do to so many of our kinsmen, or shall we do something else."

Pausing once again to let his words sink in with the group, one sailor, identity unknown spoke up. "Let's turn 'em over to the dark ones. I's hears they's eats people where they come from."

"Aye, that be fittin'", remarked another. The four freed slaves began to smile and look intently at the Spanish. Not fully understanding all that was going on the Spanish captives did, at least seem to understand this last part and began to grow exceedingly nervous at the idea that they may be turned over to former slaves.

"Aye" remarked Drake. Then addressing the assembled, but more directly the four escaped, free slaves, the Captain responded to the suggestion. "Aye, you mates are surely the most aggrieved. Certainly you men have more reason to hate than all of us combined and I do not wish to take that away from you. But as a Christian and a fellow sailor I cannot stand idly by whilst this be done. In light of that I would have to allow you four to take these prisoners ashore to do your deed. Unfortunately, if this is the course you choose, then I will not be able to hold anchor while this act is carried out, for to do so will endanger the entire command. It must also be noted that if you are to go ashore, then you will give up all hope of ever seeing your homeland again. If, however, you choose to stay onboard, I cannot promise that we will return you to your home, but I can tell you that you will have a much better chance of this happening."

With these words all fell silent only the lapping of the waves and an occasional sea bird could be heard. After what seemed to be the pause of eternity, the four Africans, without uttering a sound, angrily tossed their weapons to the deck and walked to the rear of the crowd.

With a sigh of relief, Drake continued, "alright then. Prepare the boats, we will set them adrift. We will see how good of seamen they are."

As Drake set the sailors adrift, one of their fellow Spaniards was not as benevolent to his own captives back on the other side of the continent.

The screams were blood curdling, yet undeniable. The sounds permeated throughout the hacienda and shattered the stillness of the tropical night. The servants knew, but turned their heads in denial. The constant wailing and shrieking were interrupted only by the occasional smack or cracking sounds that the whip brought. The sounds were those that stirred the soul, which you could feel in your gut. These were the noises that would normally make a grown man ashamed for inaction yet no one raced to the young slave girl's aid. For they knew, slaves to a sort, everyone, knew. Too many times in the past these sounds interrupted the night on this emerald island the visitors called Espanolá. The servants sought refuge amongst their conditions of squalor. Holding each other, they reminisced of the past, before the visitors came, before their lives had turned in to a living hell. They thought of those since departed, they were the lucky ones. They would not have to endure the backbreaking labor from sun up to sun down only to be treated to a corn paste meal and putrid water. And while they tried to digest this misery they were entertained to the sounds of some unfortunate young woman, or the occasional boy who had been chosen for a night of *company* to the Señor.

There use to be so many of their people. Friends, everyone, were now gone. These visitors spoke of a single God who was good and just, yet they acted in torture and brought filth and disease to the once pristine island that was their home. Revolts had proven fruitless against the *fire sticks* of the Spanish. And so, they were all condemned to a life of utter misery. These once noble people had now been reduced to less than half their number from when the visitors arrived. Something that they had called the "pox" seemed the most devastating. Running rampant through the native population it had eliminated entire villages, and not just on Espanolá but else where throughout New Spain. This created a severe labor shortage to work the fields and mines. So the Spanish adopted the practice, similar to the Portuguese, of the importation of slaves from Africa. These slaves seemed to be easier to control for the Spanish. This was quite possibly due to the extreme separation from home and considering that all of them had come from different areas not all could communicate with each other. But screams were screams in any language, and the unfortunate young girl that the Señor had this evening was one of these new comers of darkened skin. This one in particular del Vargas had purchased just this morning and evidently particularly for this purpose. Choosing her for her well- endowed frame, del Vargas knew that this one in particular would be vulnerable. She was alone in this New World and all that she had come into acquaintance with were sold to the mines.

It was not uncommon for the Señor to treat his "guests" this way. He was well known amongst the locals for obtaining some perverse pleasure in the torture of young women as he forced them to fulfill his sexual fantasies. Sometimes he would take an occasional boy. But whenever he did, you would not hear that much screaming, you would just never see the boy again. The natives were actually relieved with the arrival of this new group of people. The Señor seemed to like their women more, sometimes taking two or three at a time. But tonight something was wrong. It hung in the air like a mist or a stench. Tonight his torture seemed exceptional cruel. This was a cruelty that gave cause for remorse for the girl, for she could not have been more than sixteen. Her screams seemed to go on forever but finally died out when the moon had reached its highest peak for the evening.

The Spanish referred to these new people as Negro and treated them with special brutality. There was absolutely no regard for these people at all nor respect, the natives noted. At least no matter how poor their conditions grew or no amount of squalor that they were forced to live in, the natives' living conditions could never come close as to that of the darker people. During a carnival style atmosphere, the Spanish would herd these naked people like animals or chattel, chained to each other off of large ships and through the village. The stench of these poor retched souls was overwhelming. Not that they personally had a smell other than that normally expected of any other human being, but the conditions in which they were transported under created odors all of their own. For over three months these captives laid, chained together, belly-to-back, so to speak, below deck of a leaking transport across rough seas. All human secretions were deposited here, including vomit caused from the pitching and rolling of the ship. If one or two of their numbers had died in the long transit, the others, still chained to the decaying corpse would have to carry the body with them to the center of town. When they got to the center of the village, one by one the healthy ones were brought up on a platform and auctioned off. During the auction special features, good and bad were pointed out. The men seemed to take keen pleasure in this process, especially with the young girls. Attributes, such as size of breast or softness of lips gathered the most attention. Through all of this they were separated from all that they had come to know, family, friends, children from parents and siblings and then sold, one by one. And in the act of selling, each of these dark skinned people lost their life to eternal misery. Acting as a backdrop to the auction, those that had died in transit or considered being too weak or sickly for sale were thrown into the village fires and burned. The disposal process filled the small village with a putrid smell and thick smoke, accompanied by the faint screams of those that were still alive when thrown into the fires.

This practice was somewhat perplexing to the native population. The Spanish tried to tell the native population that they were not civilized and that they were heathens because they had many gods. But not one native god called for the buying or selling of another human being. Only defeated peoples, after significant battles were lost, did the natives consider taking slaves. Not this practice of marketing them and selling them so openly and without the honor of a fight. Degrading the dark skinned even more; often the slaves were branded like cattle right on the platform itself.

Just as he was covering the retching body, a knock came to his door. Del Vargas turned in surprise. Which of his servants would have the audacity to interrupt him when he was enjoying this young slave?

"Who dares to disturb me at this time of night?" bellowed del Vargas, expecting the cowering response from a servant.

And yet he was surprised by the response when it came in perfect Spanish, "I bring you a message from the Governor, Señor".

Startled del Vargas attempted to delay the messenger at the door while he covered the evidence.

"Just a minute, I'll be right there", came his hurried answer.

"Señor!" This voice was from someone different, someone much more demanding. "I will not be kept waiting at the door of my junior like some dog, open it immediately!" commanded the voice.

For this voice was not of an ordinary messenger, this was voice of the Governor's Chief Consulate, the Généralissimo Goméz. Now worried del Vargas hurried to hide the evidence of his sexual pleasures. The new territorial Governor had issued a ban on this type of activity for it was considered blasphemous.

Gaining no response from del Vargas, and after hearing the screams from afar, the Généralissimo turned to his escort and commanded, "Remove the door!" Immediately three soldiers made short order of the barrier. As the door gave way and crashed to the floor, del Vargas was startled by the noise, but no more so than by the presence of the Généralissimo.

"What moves here Señor", came the question from Goméz? "What evil do you commit? Why were we entertained in our approach by screams? Were you not informed of our late arrival"?

Del Vargas was overwhelmed with fear. He had no idea that he was to receive visitors this evening or any other evening for that matter, especially one from the Governor's office and a Généralissimo at that! If he survived the most certain coming inquisition, he would ensure, painfully so, that the servant that had failed to pass on the message would never do it again. With this thought came a smile to his face that was visible to the Généralissimo.

"You find something amusing Señor", questioned Goméz? "Is it amusing to you to keep me, Généralissimo Juan Diego de la Nunéz de Goméz waiting and not to be received in a manner suitable to my position? I shall inform the Governor of this treatment and of this condition that I find as soon as I return!"

Del Vargas was thunderstruck. He was speechless. Standing in front of the Généralissimo in utter amazement and shock, slowly del Vargas came to grips with reality.

"A thousand pardons your Eminence, for I had no idea that anyone was to visit this evening, especially someone as esteemed as you," he started with almost a hiss to his voice. "I can assure you your Excellènce that on my honor I will find the perpetrator of this crime and punish them severely. This native race rebels in unusual ways", attempting to fix blame on the natives or somewhere other than himself.

"Is your idea of severe punishment that which is evident before me, Señor? Do you know of the penalties for such activity?"

Knowing that he was seemingly caught in the act del Vargas had to think up a lie and do it quick.

"Genéralissimo I can assure you that this is not what it seems. For I have only recently returned my self. I was out on the south end of the hacienda when I heard screaming. Upon entry I found this young woman laying here. From my cursory investigation I determined that she had been ill-treated, but beyond that I have no other findings for I had only just begun to investigate when your knock arrived".

Not convinced but unwilling to lower himself any further and stoop to the obvious level of del Vargas, Goméz proceeded with the purpose of his visit.

"Señor, as I'm sure you are aware by now the Governor has named you, for reasons beyond me, to protect the shipments. The Governor has further determined that to carry out this all-important task you are ill situated, strategically of course. Therefore by the setting of the next moon you are to re-position yourself at the new colony at Saint Augustinè and take up the issue of any new foreign establishments north of there".

Turning without waiting for a response, the Genéralissimo walked towards the door. Not wishing to stay the night in the

Government hacienda as was customary; the Genéralissimo wanted to seek shelter elsewhere. As he walked to the door, reality set in and knowing full well that no other suitable place was available in this impoverished village, he reluctantly acquiesced and allowed the attentive servant to show him to his quarters.

Before leaving del Vargas, however, Goméz turned as he went through the door and stated "I will leave you with my most trusted aid to assist in your investigation. I am eagerly awaiting his report". And with that he was gone.

While del Vargas was left to contemplate his next course, Thomasin was adjusting to her new life to the other side of the world.

The sisters at the Convent were especially inhuman. That was the only term that could describe their treatment of her. Entering in as she did automatically placed three strikes against her. First she was English, spawn of the hated rulers of this territory of France for years. Barbaric rulers, that only after a two hundred-year bloody, arduous occupation, were they expelled. Second she was raised a Protestant and was now enrolled in a Catholic Convent. Protestants were considered blasphemous rebels to turn their back on the "True Church" and ultimately the Pope. Not only was she Protestant, but the subject of the rouge state whose own monarch was the bastard child from a marriage that the Pope denied! Third, she was only in the convent for education, not to take vows. This alone marked her as an outsider, an outcast. As an outsider she deserved *special* treatment, or at least this is what the sisters had conveyed to her father. Their form of "special" treatment back home was reserved for only those in the Tower, Thomasin reflected.

All girls were required to perform certain tasks every day to ensure proper order of things at the convent. Those that were pledged to vows were additionally entitled to one day of rest per week, usually Sunday. Those without the pledge of vows were not entitled to such. On the day that the "pledged" were to rest and devote to worship those not so attached were to perform all the normal tasks with the addition of those tasks assigned for "atonement." The most difficult of which was the laundry conveniently scheduled for Sunday, of course. Thomasin was required to strip all twenty-three beds, carry the heavy bedding down the stairs and out into the courtyard. Here she would have to boil the sheets in a lye soap mixture, as prescribed by the Sisters, for one hour. This in itself was difficult for the boiling of lye gave off caustic fumes that burned the eyes. Prolonged exposure, particularly with these Sunday washing chores would often render her temporarily blind, sometimes for up to two hours. And, of course, the pot that she had to use was only big enough for about half of the bedding at a time, so her task took hours to complete. Naturally, if she was to boil the sheets, this also meant that she had to draw the water from the well, which was a considerable distance away.

The well in which she drew the water was the village well, a good fifteen-minute walk one way. Given her frail and malnourished body one pail full of water was all she could manage at a time. Through the large wooden gates of the convent she would trudge, down the dusty path to the well. During the rainy season of this northern France community the path already well rutted turned to dense dark mud. As she walked down the trail the mud would squish through the holes in her worn out shoes, filling them with the cold slimy substance. The mud with a heavy mix of clay was extremely slippery. More than once she had lost her balance and fell headfirst into the quagmire. An accident such as this only meant that she would have to return to the well to refill her pail. Just filling this blasted kettle, thought Thomasin, took hours!

After completing this task, she then had to set the fire. Setting the fire was not all that difficult, as long as there was a supply of wood; which half the time that seemed to be also in short supply. Of course, this meant that she had to chop wood for the fire. Again a task that she was not well suited for, the axe was almost heavier than Thomasin. After a typical spell of chopping wood and hauling it up out of the forest, Thomasin's hands would be ripped, raw and bleeding. The sting of the lye soap when it hit these hands would bring tears to her eyes. With tear filled eyes the caustic in the lye would intensify its burn. *What Christian charity they display,* mused Thomasin. Thomasin's mind wondered as it often did, *if I ever get out of here, and marry, I certainly wouldn't choose a churchgoer!*

Those that were *pledged* were entitled to fulfill themselves with the fruits that God provided. All others were considered "unworthy to even clean the scraps from the bountiful harvest".

This stipulation in the Convent order translated to be those with *pledges* ate first; those without could clear the table, and clean up after meals. Often she would be interrupted from her drudgery of laundry just to clean up after the *pledged* ate. If there was anything left over, she could consume it or give it to the dogs. Only, of course after her other chores were complete. Even with this, sometimes the sisters felt it necessary to feed the dogs first; especially if her chores lasted longer than planned.

It was in these early days of Convent life that were the worst for Thomasin and it was in these early days that, Thomasin had the unfortunate occasion to meet a young Frier recently assigned to the Convent named Jean LePere. He was almost frail in appearance; creepy, actually Thomasin considered him, more than Godly. He could be often seen from a distance watching the younger girls which gave Thomasin an ill feeling about him well before he started brushing up against her. Too often it seemed to be by chance he would brush up against her or would want to sit beside her during evening mass. Sometimes this even meant squeezing in where it was most inappropriate to do so, causing others to loose their seat on the end of the row, which, of course, made the underlying animosity towards Thomasin grow worse! When she finally complained to one of the Sisters, Thomasin was told that it was she that was sinful and who was having sinful thoughts!

The weeks stretched into months. Phases of the moons passing, but always her mother remained in her thoughts. She was so lonely, forgotten and beyond depression to the point of despair. She had already tried taking her life but was unsuccessful even in that. That in itself was dreadful! It earned her a whipping that she would not soon forget and a return to the very person that had driven her to attempt the act to start with. The chain of events for this particular occasion occurred after an event that was natural for all young girls to go through, the first menstruation. The sisters considered it as a sign that the *Devil* was with this child, for Thomasin had hers early in the eyes of the Convent. Mother Superior relied upon her most trusted agent. So, it was not that much of a surprise when the task fell to LePere.

For this simple natural act, one beyond her control, the Frier, himself, had the dubious task of whipping her, possibly out of choice and only after she had been placed in the stocks and striped. Here she was a young girl of thirteen, whipped and stripped, alone, for the sisters had already departed…then the Frier had his way.

The next day is when she attempted to take her life. At a point of total despair, Thomasin had cried all night. Not being able to clean and wash him out, she had been violated and now had to remain so. His fluid mixed with blood trickled down her leg, staining her garments for permanent display. Who was she to tell? Wasn't religion grand? Wasn't it amazing how the true scum of this world, the defilers of the innocent, deviants all, could actually hide behind the guise of religion? No wonder people rebelled, or started the "Protestant" movement, to protest the abuses of the Church. Now she just hoped against hope that this particular Frier, after periods of supposed celibacy, was unfertile. *Hope?* Even the word now was empty. This place was barren of hope. The Church was supposed to be the pillar of hope to the world. And yet its servant is the one that had caused her plunge into hell. Why was this done to her? Why was she cast into this plight? Why had her own father been so shortsighted as to think she would be better off here than at home? What truly was behind his thought that committed this act of treachery and sentenced her to this torture? Searching but not finding any answers to these questions, Thomasin attempted to end her life. She tied a few bed linens together and after securing them to the third floor stair rail in a huge double knot she tied the other end around her neck. Slowly she climbed to the top of the stair rail. As she stood there looking down to the stone entrance way below, she thought of her mother and the days in Auld together. Tears came to her eyes because she knew that she would never see her mother again.

The other girls were just returning from prayer. As they made their way up the long winding staircase, the lead girl noticed Thomasin standing on the rail. Calling out to her in French, the girl questioned if Thomasin had finished her chores. Not really understanding what the girl said, Thomasin turned and looked her in the eye and threw herself off the rail. The sudden stop in her plunge at the end of the linen was enough to rip the lye damaged bed sheets in half sending her to the stone floor below. The bed sheets were too large around her neck to suffocate her but had provided just enough force to slow her decent so that when she hit the stone floor below with nothing broken.

For this act, rather than counseling and confession, she was rewarded with yet another whipping at the hands of the same Frier. When he was through, he again had his way.

How many times now had it been that the Frier Jean visited? Each time he would come after dark, silently creeping into her bed. She attempted to fight him off, but with every struggle his desire would intensify. Smelling of boiled meat and Communion wine he would slobber and lick her face with every push and grunt. She remembered twice, but was there more? She really did not want to know. She only prayed that she would be barren.

Solace from her plight came with the arrival of Esmeralda. She was a dark haired beauty that stood a good three inches more than Thomasin. Judging from her appearance, however, Thomasin felt that they were probably about the same age. Although she had the color of a stiff cup of tea, her eyes were big and a bright green. What a wonderful mix thought Thomasin as she looked upon Esmeralda. Brief introductions were made and then Thomasin set about the seemingly arduous task of establishing some form of communication. Speaking in broken French, mixed with a little Spanish and a crude form of sign language thrown in for good measure, neither girl was successful at first. Undeterred in their quest, both girls sought out other forms. Soon, by working together, they were able to communicate by using a form of language that was a hybrid of English and Esmeralda's native tongue. French was used sparingly and usually only when the sisters were near. Although Esmeralda knew more French than English, the latter was the obvious choice of Thomasin.

Like the English occupation forces in this region before her, Thomasin had refused to learn any more French than she absolutely had too. The attitude towards learning the local language was the same as expressed by those soldiers that had occupied the region for so many years. This viewpoint had long been a hallmark of the English culture. Members of the Order found it quite interesting that it manifested itself in such a young child. The attitude radiated from Thomasin like an aurora and was evident in every aspect of her actions, thought, word and deed. The attitude was one that the sisters found intolerable and bound them to the charge of exercising it from her soul. This was the attitude of English arrogance and it spoke of a common thought amongst all English. The thought most associated with it was one of *"I am English the rest of you are inferior and if you wish to communicate with me, then by God you will have the decency to learn English."* Born with an air of self-righteous arrogance, nothing seemed to ease the situation. Rather, Thomasin resigned herself to the fact that it was not one she could divorce herself from. After all, she was a proper English lady and these were mere continental peasants resigned to some perverse religious order that had abused the rights of mankind for centuries!

The language that the girls developed contained numerous native words as well, with the slight touch of French so as to ward off any suspicion. The two ended up sharing everything, from the numerous chores to crusts of bread and the occasional piece of meat. The meat was usually taken by teamwork from the dogs.

After a while Thomasin learned that Esmeralda was the daughter of a half-French half-Spanish sea trader. Her mother was that of a native breed from New Spain. Her father had met and married her mother on one of many trips to the New

World. Her name, Esmeralda, was given to her to help her blend in with the Spanish, but it didn't seem to work. With her mothers passing from the "pox" Esmeralda was placed in the care of her grandmother. Her grandmother being of proper French stock and a Catholic had neither room nor desire to raise another child in her advanced years. Coupled with the thought that the union between Esmeralda's mother and father was *unholy*, for it occurred outside of the Church, Esmeralda was considered a bastard. When her father left her with her grandmother for rearing and returned to the sea; Esmeralda was quickly turned over to the sisters at the Convent.

Both outcast and alone in the world, the two girls quickly became closer than any friend could ever be. As they shared tasks they each taught something of their own past; culture, language, customs…whatever they could to pass the time and to remember. The months passed and soon it was harvest time. For most, this was a time of joy and anticipation for the coming of winter. Most homes, as well as here in the Convent, smells of cooking and preserving of food for the winter permeated the air. The green grass had long since given way to the rich; multi- colored leaves of autumn. These were unusual sights for Esmeralda and as such it was a particularly trying time for her. She was already ill with the croup. The almost certain coming of cooler weather did not bode well for her. Originating in warmer climates she was not used to the cold and had never seen snow! It was not long before Esmeralda's condition grew worse. It started with an increasing croup attached to the development of a yellow-ish mucus that she would spit up with almost every hacking cough. The problem or illness slowly migrated to a low-grade fever marked with periods of cold chills.

Now it was customary throughout Europe that at this time of year most school children would return home to their family for the winter months. This helped ease the burden of feeding the girls and reduced the requirements to heat the schools and the amount of crops that would have to be grown to sustain them over the winter. To make the necessary arrangements, the Sisters were very careful to instruct the girls to transcribe letters to their families. These were done, however, under the ever-watchful eye of the Order. Each letter was reviewed for *spelling*, but as Thomasin mused, it was more to ensure the truth was not known outside these walls. Draft letters were prepared by all save Esmeralda, for she had no one to write to. When Thomasin saw this, she naturally had to ask her friend why.

"Esmeralda, why don't you prepare a letter to your grandmamma" she questioned.

"She does not want me, she thinks me an animal", replied her friend.

Appalled at the response and finding it difficult to believe that anyone, especially a relation could hold such an opinion of their own flesh and blood, Thomasin was dumbfounded.

"No" she said expressing an element of shock rarely used. "I'm sure you misunderstood her," exclaimed Thomasin.

"Thank you, my friend, but you are wrong. I understood very well. She used my people's word".

Shaking her head in continued disbelief Thomasin attempted to console her friend and said "fine then you shall come with me to England!"

"Oh Thomasin, you mean it" shocked and surprised all at once; Esmeralda was so overcome at the suggestion that she nearly broke out in tears. "Do you think that they would want someone like me" she questioned?

"Esmeralda" Thomasin responded, "Not everyone are like these people. If I ask, my mother will care for you as she does for me."

"You mean it! But what about your father, how will he respond" Esmeralda inquired.

"Don't mind him, he doesn't like anyone!"

Both girls broke out into laughter, which brought the immediate wrath of the Sisters to quell the disturbance. With heads held low, Thomasin and Esmeralda looked at each other, smiled, letting out a muffled girlish giggle and prepared the letter.

Despite being sick, Esmeralda had to continue with her daily chores. Thomasin tried to take some of the burden off her friend but most of the time the sisters would put a stop to it and just assign more to Esmeralda. Normally this was done under the guise that Esmeralda was just lazy and was attempting to portray illness so her friend would take on more of the work. Both girls knew that this was not the case. This illness or condition would not go away by itself. And it did not help that the girls were both forced to sleep in the damp basement. Their bedding was more of a pallet made from straw that had a tendency to take on the moisture from the surrounding room. The room itself was perennially damp and cold, even in the summer months. It was originally designed to be a wine and *root cellar* and therefore possessed few windows and had large granite walls designed to retain the cool moist evening air.

As the winter months set in, all of the girls, *pledged* and *un-pledged* alike looked forward to returning home. Often evening chatter amongst the girls was occupied with words of home, each girl trying to convince her audience that she had the best life. Excitement and anticipation was heavy and filled the air like a dense fog along the coast. The conditions in the basement, although deteriorating rapidly due to the dropping temperature, were no less exciting despite already being able to see ones breath. The winter also meant even less to eat. Subsistence consisted primarily of Thomasin's now *famous* butter and sugar sandwiches. This was something that Thomasin had acquired a taste for several months previously. Bread was always plentiful, as too butter. Sugar was a little harder, but the bread was filling and something that even the dogs were not tremendously fond of, so there was always some thing left in their bowls. The two of them had withered to less than half the size of young girls of similar age. The shortage of nutrition and hygiene standards had reduced their normal development. This actually, as Thomasin reflected was a good thing, a blessing in disguise, for the Priest no longer found her attractive! Hygiene…Oh to take a bath…how long had it been Thomasin thought? Her and her mother would take a bath in heather and rose water at least twice a month. She had already been here in purgatory for some eight months now without so much as a wash down!

Unbeknownst to Thomasin, Esmeralda suffered from another affliction; an affliction that robbed a person of the meager nourishment that they received. Close to the time that the girls anticipated going home all they could speak of was the joy of being free from this place. However, before the girls were to depart, on one fateful day near what the French called Yuletide, her affliction would manifest itself. Yuletide, a holiday recognized by almost everyone in Europe but unknown to Esmeralda. Thomasin explained that it was pagan in origin, but conveniently related to the coming of Christ and the Christian holiday of Christmas.

While sharing a butter and sugar sandwich in their basement hubble after a particularly hard day, Esmeralda started to cough which by now had become quite common place. But her coughing got worse and was soon followed by choking and gagging as if she were going to draw at any moment her last breath. Gasping and retching, grabbing her throat she started acting as if she was going to unleash her insides and regurgitate her merger meal of bread. Startled, Thomasin did not know what to do. She attempted to bring her water but was pushed away. She attempted to beat her on the back, which she had seen many times before in a similar situation, but this did not help. Both girls were terrified not knowing what was going to transpire. Petrified Thomasin called for the sisters in an attempt to help her friend. Just as one of the sisters arrived, Esmeralda was in a final gasp and cough. Then out of the mouth it came, a snake like or worm-like thing as big as one's forearm! Esmeralda had coughed up a tapeworm! This, of course, was a true sign of their plight. A tapeworm will only exit itself from the host if the host has nothing more to offer. Shrieking, shaking and to the point of utter panic both girls ran for the door. In their haste one of them, culprit unknown, ran into the sister who had come to the aid of their screams. When the sister was struck, she was caught off balance and fell backwards striking her head on the corner of the wooden stairs. The girls, in a state of panic kept running and soon they were beyond the walls of the convent.

The girls ran the best they could off into the cold night, not knowing of their fate. But, fate always has a way of making itself known even when it pertains to the decisions of Royalty.

"**B**ut, begging the Excellence pardon, but to wage war and attack another sovereign nation prior to exercising all other options…. well just seems too English."

The admiral knew that his suggestion would not be received well at all by the Monarch. He had to try, however. Upon uttering his suggestion the room fell silent as all present looked at King Philip, waiting for the explosive response that all had assured themselves would follow. After a pause that seemed endless, the King slowly rose from his chair and walked across the room to his desk. Opening the draw he pulled out parchment and began to write instructions. As the others looked on, the room was as silent as a tomb. Would Spain attack England? Was the King preparing yet another excursion? Could Spain continue to expand and draw its forces even more thin?

Suddenly, breaking the silence the admiral spoke again. Considering he was already exposed with his earlier expressed viewpoint he figured he had nothing else to loose. Bowing and presenting himself in accordance with tradition, he spoke again. "Your Majesty, the *Cacafuego* was under the command of my only son who, by now is certainly lost. If anyone would have reason to be vengeful, tis I. But even with my most certain loss, I beg you for restraint. Our forces are loyal to you, your Majesty. Your wish is our command, but I beg you for this restraint. We are too thin at present to take on an additional operation such as this size. To attack and defeat the English would be a massive undertaking and one that would pitch our forces on to that godforsaken island for years to come! Additionally Sire, I fear that to be successful our assets are not in the correct position."

As his words drifted off back into silence, the Monarch completed his draft, seal the parchment with the royal seal and rose. Smiling at the outspoken admiral, the King simply placed his hand on the overtly nervous commander. "Your words are well placed Don Hédre. Fear not, for you are correct. Rather than attack and crush this rouge state, prudence must prevail. I will send my most trusted Emissary to deliver this message to their Crown. I want my treasure returned and for the scoundrel that took it, his head in a basket! Dependent upon her response, that shall dictate our next course of action."

Relieved at these words the admiral and the rest of the advisors bowed and departed.

Meanwhile, as the fate of one suspected scoundrel was up for debate, two more would-be scoundrels of sorts discussed their potential leaps to fortune.

"One of the ships is due in with the tide at the end of the week", said Henry who had just returned to the *hole* from taking back Smitty's horse. This duty fell to Henry because he was not as well known on the wharf and that the incident this morning was still too fresh in everyone's mind. "'Ow we going to pinch it" the young boy asked? "Are we breakin' in?"

"No" came Tristan's response, "we ain't breakin' in, we bustin' out!"

"Bustin' 'ut, I don't understand" the young boy was puzzled?

"Its simple mate, we go to the Customs as marines and 'ide during the day we do, then 'fter they close for the night, we come out and have all the time we want to shop" laughed Tristan! "The treasures of Kings meant for a Queen. We will have all the quid we want to fix Mum and buy us new clothes as well. Hell maybe we buy everyone some new clothes, ey"?

The boys were laughing hard now and could hardly wait to make their score. Putting his arm around his young companion, Tristan and Henry walked out the opening to the *hole* and proceeded down the alley.

"Let's get something to eats" signed Tristan, as the two would-be thieves skipped merrily down the rain soaked alley, pausing occasionally to splash in convenient puddles.

Their gait steadily increased, as each boy enjoyed attempting to tag the other as they ran through the back streets. The boys chased each other through the area named Tower Hamlets. This name was attached to the small dwellings surrounding the Tower and dated back to the time of the Roman invasion. After the dissolution of the Monasteries that had pocked this portion of the city, the area started a period of revival and industrialization. Already signs of the *higher social order* started to appear.

Now breathless Tristan remarked to his younger companion, "it 'on't be long before we's ain't welcomed 'ere!"

"Why's that Duke" questioned Henry.

"See's that over there" pointing to the construction of a new studio and dwelling where a portion of the old monastery once stood.

"Aye. What's that got's to do with us?"

"That's the sign of the rich movin' into our space, that is. Won't be long before they bring the law 'ere and run us off. It's always the way. As soon as the rich folk think we's got somethin' they's takes it", explained Tristan.

Arriving outside of one of the last remaining Pubs in the area, Henry inquired, "what's we doing 'ere"?

"We's going to dine likes gentlemen, we will" replied Tristan. "We's need to get used to it".

With a puzzled look Henry followed his friend through the door. Upon entry the two boys took up a convenient table on the back wall and in the shadows. "By weeks out we will eat like this for the rest of our time", concluded Tristan.

At that point he clutched his chest to make a "locket check" and waved for the young waitress to come over. She could not have been much older than Tristan yet work at this Pub must have already taken its toll on her. Haggard looking and unkempt the girl still possessed the vivacious nature of youth and had still a spark in her eye. As she bounded on over, Tristan watched intently while stroking his chin. He had known this girl for quite sometime and had always been interested, yet never to the point of action. Their relationship was beyond platonic and more of cat and mouse. Changing barbs at each other, both displayed that level of attention and desire that if left alone time would soon blossom.

"We's like some 'ggs and fried pork, we do" Tristan ordered up.

"'Ave's you got some money, sir", questioned the girl? "By's the look of ye I should runs you 'ut of'ere!"

Reaching across the table and grabbing Henry's shoulder in a form of brotherly friendship, Tristan laughed, "Ourse we's do shrew, why's you thunk we's come 'ere. Now be off with you's or you ain't get no tip from us!"

"A tip, from you's…why you's be lucky to pay what's owed!"

And with that remark the girl turned with a huff and pranced away with their order.

"Have you's lost it mate! Where's the blooming money" exclaimed Henry!

"Tut, tut me wee little tot" replied Tristan. "Today we eats as gentlemen, for soon we is!"

With that remark both boys started their laughter all over again.

"But 'ows we going to pay now?" Henry could not let the subject just drop away. Although Henry was young he was not as foolhardy as most his age.

"I pinched more than one bag of coin last night on the wharf" chuckled Tristan. "That's where I was and why you, my weasel, 'ad to go on to check the ships", said Tristan and with that, slapping Henry once again on the shoulder.

"You's mean from the fat one at the seconds store", questioned Henry?

"Natch" quipped Tristan.

"Blimy" exclaimed Henry, 'e's the mean one, you shouldn't mess with 'im. I's hear that he' s kin to the guards' at Customs. No wonder you's was late."

"No matter" said Tristan. "His money spends just as well" again laughing. He wondered looking around to see if anyone was looking. They would probably think that he was drunk, except it was early even by street life standards, if there was such a thing. "Still," touching his chest, Tristan thought to himself and yet concentrating so hard that he actually spoke the same words, he had that creepy, skin crawling kind of feeling that only occurs when you are being watched…but by whom?

"When you checked the ships, did you encounter anyone" questioned Tristan.

"Only a friendly watchman. He thinks me from London School and be lost. I fooled him so well, he 'elped me" replied Henry.

This started the boys laughing all over again.

Unbeknownst to Tristan, Lieutenant Harvey Anson had finally won the High Commanders permission, which was quite an undertaking in its own right. As with all good officers the Lieutenant had to serve in a variety of duty positions in order to establish a *well-rounded* career. Part of this was the service for fourteen months as the Wharf Constable, or Wharf Provost in military terms. Lieutenant Harvey Anson had served this position well but never to the point that would mark his career as he had hoped. He had never established that one big case or event. With his tour nearly complete, Anson was looking for the *big one* that one singular event that would surely mark his career as a success. For well over a year now Anson had been petitioning the High Command of the Military District of London for the right to wear common street clothes and move amongst the crowd undetected. This *detection* work as Anson referred to it as, was seen as a cowardly way of conducting the Queen's business. And as such the High Command was reluctant to authorize one of their officers to conduct business in this manner. They considered it to be related to that of a *spy* in battle. To be a spy and out of uniform was a hanging offense. "How could being a spy on the wharf be any different?" was often the response. Then it happened. A band of rouge youngsters moved into the wharf area during Anson's watch. They prayed not only on the business owner but the patrons as well. Business started to suffer and it was soon after that the High Command finally authorized Anson's suggestion. They gave him a fortnight to prove that his methods were to be of use.

On this eighth day of dressing as a street person and taking one meal at the local establishment, Anson was about to have his efforts pay huge dividends. Although Tristan and Henry were in the shadows, they were in the *clear view* of the Lieutenant; who was concealed to them. The young girl who performed duties as waitress, amongst others, had been well reimbursed for her services by the dashing Lieutenant. These services included the occasional passing of information on the activities of the various patrons. The gracious Provost adequately supplemented her meager wage from the Pub, and therefore he commanded her *loyalty.* This level of service to the dashing stranger was not affected by her concealed feelings for Tristan.

The boys had caught the Lieutenant's eye and suspicion. These two were common street rats. The larger one fit the description rendered by the shoppe owner. These two seemed happy enough yet out of place, even for a place like this. *So, why were they here*, Anson thought. This Pub or Establishment was certainly a vial place suitable for the likes of them, or anyone else that would rather slice your throat then say G'day…but why were these two young boys so boisterous and able to buy food? This may be of interest, pondered the Lieutenant. From his vantage point he could see a small purse on the table before them. From the distance, however, he could not make out the details well enough to mark identification. Small purse, dark in color, *"Umm…"* wondered Anson. As he tapped his forefinger to his lips Anson drifted deep in thought. *"I wonder if it has the markings of "C.J.S." as the shoppe owner claimed from this morning?"* he thought. *"I wonder, could it be my lucky day or is this mere coincidence",* he continued in his train of thought. The more he thought and watched the two boys, the more he had to get a better look. Ever since Sand Hurst, he had never turned down an offer of challenge or fail in mission.

So calling her back to his table, Anson offered the young waitress two crowns, which she gleefully accepted; remarking that "'d sell me Mum for such a Kingly sum, who'd I have to kill?"

"Just look at the purse over there with those two lads, motioning across the room with a flick of his wrist, and tell me what you see."

Not soon after the girl delivered their order of eggs and fried pork. There on the table before her laid the purse, from which Tristan pulled several gold coins to pay the wench. In closing the purse with an audible "snap" Tristan made visible the front side. She could clearly see the markings of "C.J.S." in gold letter print. Without reaction the girl collected the coins, securing her tip from the rest, and thanked them appropriately. With a "I'll see you's later" she scampered off. Causing Tristan to blush at the remark, she secured her intent. Unsuspectingly, Tristan and Henry dug in with gusto to their hearty feast. When the Lieutenant's meal was ready the girl delivered it as well, at which time she rendered her report.

"The purse, sir, has the markings of C.J.S. in gold letters on the front it do."

"Fine, thank you. Now here's your coin, and be off with you."

Now the Lieutenant had something of interest. But, of course he could not make an arrest on this information alone. Certainly if he tried the lads would soon gain a barrister who would question whether they had found the purse or had obtained it.

Wiping his utensils prior to use, for he did not trust the cleanliness of the Establishment, he sliced his pork and chewed on it slowly. Pondering his next move as carefully as a chess player, Anson slowly ate his meal. Wonder what my life would have been if it weren't for the family business he thought so intently he almost uttered the words. Anson was the grandson of the famous weapons manufacturer and as such he had been born to a level of wealth that would have ordinarily kept him from service. But being a young man and always looking for adventure, Harvey joined the Royal Marines against his father's wishes. Thinking still, Anson pondered the question. Then adding to it, *"What would it be like to be one of those boys? Were they born here or simply migrated like so many of the others? In the midst of such poverty and filth, what could be so amusing that these two could continue to laugh and carry on as such? There has got to be more than just this purse…but what?"*

The scene at the Pub continued on until Anson had finished. Rising slowly as to not cast suspicion, he paid his fare and proceeded out the side entrance as causally as if he had done this a hundred times. After returning to his quarters, washing, for it was always good to have the filth of the streets off of him, he changed into his crimson and white uniform of the Royal Marines. When suited for duty, Lieutenant Anson departed his quarters and marched briskly down the wharf to the Provost Office, which was conveniently situated at the entrance to the main docking platform and Customs House. The door was already unlocked which was customary for Sergeant Bristol was an early riser. As he entered the office, he could see Sergeant Bristol handing out today's mission sheets to three of the junior ranking Marines. At almost the instant that Lieutenant Anson's boot struck the wood plank floor, Sergeant Bristol called the room to attention by announcing "Officer on deck!" and immediately bringing his heels of his well polished knee-high boots together with a loud click. The other three responded in similar fashion and just as smartly.

"Carry on" commanded the Lieutenant. "Sergeant Bristol, when you have a moment I need to see you, in private".

"Aye-aye Sir!"

Then turning to his men assembled in front of him Sergeant Bristol commanded "that will be all men, fall-out". And with that, the good sergeant marched the best he could across the room to the Lieutenant. Sergeant Bristol had joined the Royal Marines at the ripe age of fourteen. He had seen countless action from the Scots up north to the French overseas. His last several years had been in Drake's Squadron as they *policed* the sea. Which was the term used to describe the pirating of Spanish gold shipments. Although Drake was not an "official" member of Her Majesty's Navy, he served in a capacity that was sanctioned by the Crown. As such, it was not unusual for the vessels under Drake's command to have a contingent of Royal Marines on board. With *special* licensing arrangements the fledging Navy could be financed in part through investments from wealthy business owners and barons. These *arrangements* provided much needed funds to finance his expeditions and equip his ships for the long sea voyages, while not directly linking the Crown to his escapades.

It was in this capacity that the Sergeant first encountered the fresh Lieutenant from Sand Hurst. Assigned to bring the *Green L.T.* along Sergeant Bristol and Lieutenant Anson struck up a relationship that was almost father and son. The love of the sea was visible in his eyes, and yet he could no longer return. On his last voyage Sergeant Bristol had been gravely wounded in the upper right thigh by Spanish musket fire. He was, at one time, in danger of loosing his leg for the fear of infection, but then the Lieutenant interceded on his behalf. With the Lieutenant's considerable wealth and fondness for the Sergeant, a suitable surgeon was found. This surgeon was able to save the leg, thus indebting the good Sergeant to the Lieutenant's service. Ever since then the Sergeant walked with a considerable limp, however, which precluded him from even walking quickly let alone run and therefore condemned him to shore duty.

"Sergeant Bristol", began the Lieutenant "aren't you from here originally", came the question?

The Lieutenant never forgot a detail Sergeant Bristol thought. "Aye sir, less than a few blocks from 'ere. Begging the sir's pardon, why's 'ou ask?"

"You do then still have acquaintances here then don't you?" asked Anson, already knowing the answer. The Lieutenant loved to play a form of mental chess and this line of questioning already was starting to wear thin on the Sergeant. The Sergeant's uneasiness soon began to show through as his superior was addressing him.

"Aye sir, but ye already's knows this? Why's the question?"

"Sergeant, do you know Charles Slidell, the second's goods dealer?"

"Aye sir, I was employed by 'im in me younger days. Good man, fine merchant, always a kind word. Never turned down a chance to 'elp the needy he do"….

The Sergeant would have continued save the Lieutenant's cutting him off. "Fine, fine then did you know that he was relieved of a considerable sum of coin this morning?" asked the Lieutenant.

"I heard something to that affect, yes sir."

"Good, I believe that I may have a fix on where his money went and who took it but I need your help, or more appropriately, the help of your childhood companions. Are you willing to assist?"

"Aye sir but 'ous knows how the Admiralty feels 'bout that sort of thing."

The Sergeant was referring to the expression of the Admiralty or the High Command on locals that they considered to be riff-raff. Any connection with these sorts, to the honor of the Office of Provost was considered to be ungentlemanly and against the code of ethics for the officer rank. This line of thinking was directly linked to the same line that had limited Anson's ability to function in the manner that he felt he needed to operate in the *detective* mode. Considering the High Command had finally granted permission to dress in street clothes, but for only a fortnight, Anson believed that lifting this vale of standards was adaptable to other situations as well.

"I understand that Sergeant, but I will take full responsibility. Are you willing to help?"

"Aye sir, you can count on me, always can, what do you need me to do?"

"First" started the Lieutenant; "I need you to question the good shoppe owner as to whom he was chasing. I need to know if he got a good look at the rat. I have a frail description so I need him to fill in the holes. Second, quiz your friends. I need to know whom these two boys are that have been hanging around as of late. One is tall, about up to my shoulder and real skinny. He looks to be about fourteen to sixteen years of age and has dirty brown hair, shoulder length, and matted down with filth, always hangs in his eyes. His clothes are tattered and torn and wears a rope for a belt to hold up his britches. He appears to have a bad heart or something wrong with his lungs. He can be seen periodically clutching his chest. As for his companion, he is quite the younger. This one is about seven or eight years; short and thin with dirty blonde hair and again shoulder length, hanging in his eyes. Find out all you can about these two rouges, what they are up to, do they work for someone and where is their lair."

"Aye-aye sir," in typical Marine fashion. Saluting with the open palm to the near center of the forehead, as was customary and then turning, the Sergeant marched out the door. Excited about the mission that laid before him the Sergeant wasted no time in contacting his acquaintances.

Sitting back in his chair the Lieutenant decided to settle into the day's work. Just then the orderly appeared at the hatchway. The Royal Marines had a tendency to refer to everything in ships terms whether they were on land or not. This was more, sometimes out of pride in service to make them distinct and to annoy the other land service…the army.

"Request permission to enter sir," the orderly said.

"Granted" came the reply.

Marching across the room the orderly presented himself before the seated Lieutenant. Coming to the position of attention the orderly rendered the appropriate salute and stated, "Morning report sir!"

"Thank you Jenson", came the reply followed by a returned salute.

"Sir will you be takin' your customary tea and crumpets this morning" asked the orderly for it was his station in service to care for the Lieutenant.

Not an ordinary position for a Lieutenant to have in the Royal Marines but one that came with the Office of Provost. "No Jenson, just tea, thank you" came the response.

"Aye-aye sir" stated Jenson saluting and turning away. As Jenson was moving to the galley to bring the tea to his charge, he thought that the Lieutenant was acting a bit strange as of late.

For nearly the past two weeks he was not eating breakfast, not even a morsel. Such strange behavior, but then again *he was an officer* and they were a strange lot all on their own he thought. "No matter", muttered Jenson to himself, "more for me".

Looking over the Morning Report, which was only, called the Morning Report because the Provost received it in the morning. In actuality it was a report rendered from the night watchman from the previous evening. Scanning through the report all seemed to be in order. Then on page three at about mid evening after all the wharf shoppes and businesses were all closed save the Pub, Anson noticed an intriguing entry. Here nestled between the postings of the appointed rounds laid the entry. "Whilst moving from station three to station four on the south wharf, I encountered what seemed to be a lost child. He claimed to be from London School." This was a newly erected school for boys in town that had been built using primarily funds from the local merchants. It was designed to help ease the suffering of the poor by providing them with an education and training in the trades. The report continued, "The lad seemed quite friendly as I approached and asked for directions home, which I promptly gave. I escorted the lad off the wharf. He seemed to be in poor shape coming from the school and his clothes were those of a street child. The other curious thing, he inquired as to the arrival of the ships for the week, especially those late arrivals of Drake's command." The report then drifted off into other details of the evening with nothing else to being of particularly noteworthy.

"JENSON!" shouted the Lieutenant.

Almost immediately the orderly Jenson appeared at the hatchway. "Yes sir" he replied.

"Fetch me the night watch that completed this report."

"Aye-aye sir" came the Marine's response. Saluting and moving out smartly without question, as was the Marine way.

"We will see about this, lads' interest in the ships" mused Anson.

Sister Nadine was the first on the scene. As she stood atop the stair well and peered through the dim light offered by the lonely candle she held up high, Sister Nadine called out in French, "Sister Jacquelyn? Are you there? Petite chèvre?" Petite chèvre is how she was always addressed and never understood by Thomasin. Little did Thomasin know that this meant little goat in French and no one ever bothered to tell her the translation.

Thomasin was rather suspicious of the term, however, because every time some one used it the younger girls would smile or openly snicker. Based on this reaction, Thomasin knew that the term was not one of endearment.

"Are you there? Someone answer!" Gaining no response, Sister Nadine knew that she must descend the steep stairway. This was not a task that she particularly enjoyed, even in the daylight. The Reverend Mother said that was because Sister Nadine was not yet a true believer and that if she were then this stairway and the subsequent dark hole that lied ahead would not appear so ominous to her for God would provide and protect. Normally after this little speech is when the Reverend Mother would break into the Twenty-third Psalm, which is exactly what Nadine started to do as she went down the staircase. Grasping the slick stair rail in one trembling hand and holding on to the candle with the other, Sister Nadine slowly made her way down the staircase. The damp, cool air of the basement seemed to wrap around her like a cloak. The wet stairs caused footing in her leather bottomed house shoes to be treacherous, which only magnified her fear. Still repeating the Psalm as she neared the bottom of the staircase, a figure started to come into view. Through the dim light of the lonely candle, Nadine could scarcely make out the dark clothing of a nun's habit! As she approached, Nadine was able to make out the shape more clearly, it was Sister Jacquelyn! Putting her fears aside Nadine rushed to the aid of her friend, "Jacquelyn, Jacquelyn" she cried forgetting the more formal address.

Jacquelyn and Nadine had entered the Convent at approximately the same time period and over the years had become very close, Jacquelyn, the elder had supplanted the motherly figure that Nadine had so desperately still clung to.

"Reverend Mother, Father Tomas!" cried Nadine.

She knew that her friend needed more help than she was able to give at present given her emotional state and the fact that her own medical training was not yet complete. "Father Tomas" she continued.

Father Tomas was one of several Priests that were assigned to the Convent and responsible for advanced medical support and training. He was an older gentleman, who, on appearance could have been mistaken for one of noble class of Northern Italy. He often cared for the poor and sick in the village below the Convent, returning each evening to his quarters not far from the stairwell entrance.

"Reverend Mother!"

Soon other members of the Order arrived and started to lend Nadine assistance. By now Nadine was overcome with emotion and was more in the way than she was of any support. Several others helped to lift Sister Jacquelyn up the stairwell to a more lighted and comfortable area. The Reverend Mother pushed her way through the crowd of young ladies now assembled. When she made her way to the fallen sister it was immediately apparent that Sister Jacquelyn was beyond much hope. Assuming the worst, the Reverend Mother started the last rites fitting a nun of Jacqueline's stature. Almost in unison the others followed suit realizing the Reverend Mother knew what was best. By time Father Tomas arrived, it was over. Noting that by her condition she had been the victim of a head trauma and a broken neck, Father Tomas suggested that she might have died actually by the rough transport up the stairwell. Counseling the Sisters, which were gathered before him, Father Tomas suggested that they should have left her where she lay until his arrival. Quick to the defense, the Reverend Mother interjected that the girls only brought the body up the stairs and that death had been the blow to the back of the skull. Looking blankly at the Reverend Mother and then glancing around the room at the shocked faces, he realized that there was nothing to gain by being *scientific* so he nodded in agreement and rendered his professional opinion.

"Death, it seems, was caused by a blow to the back of the skull. This, of course, is the undeniable suggestion that we have a *meurtrier* or murderer in our amidst" speaking rather matter-of-factly to the assembled group of the order.

At this suggestion some of the younger pledges gasped in fright. Quickly scanning the assembled group the Reverend Mother sought to control the situation and console her flock.

"We must notify the magistrate immediately" she commanded. "The perpetrators are at large in the community. In their demonic state there is no telling what they will resort to. We must find them at once!"

And so the Sisters went out across the French country-side in search for the vile young ones, whilst events were developing anew for Drake on the other side of the world.

With treasure now secured onboard the Hind and after those that were set afloat were out-of-sight, Drake set his course. First to the west, then to the north. Crossing the 48th parallel he found safe harbor in a land that was cool, lush and enchanting. The expedition came to rest far from the heat of the tropics and amongst the largest trees that any had ever seen, to include the Africans. The trees stood taller than the largest ship and were of such magnitude that they blocked out the sun. Huge in base, it required nearly twenty men holding hand-in-hand to complete its circumference.

Making a temporary shelter at the base of one of these mighty works of God, Drake set about ensuring the necessary repairs were made to his ship. For five weeks the men lived in the forest of these giants and drew forage from the abundant wild life and plants.

Time drew near when the expedition would have to once again set sail. Just before dusk, which came early in the forest, the First Mate rapped on the outer trunk of his Captain's makeshift home.

"Hello Geoffrey, what brings you over this evening" questioned Drake.

"I come to render me latest report" responded Geoffrey.

Over the course of the long voyage the two men had become good friends. Living as they had, however, for the past several weeks in this emerald green forest far removed from everything that all had ever known the friendship grew more intense. So much so that the proverbial pleasantries of title were no longer issued or required.

"So how is it looking" questioned Drake.

"We be fine. These mighty giants have provided sturdy planking and a good steady mast. The wood is soft to the knife but once wet it seems to harden, as if God weren't done with it yet. The men have gathered plenty of food stores from the forest and I fear that soon they will grow fat and not wish to leave."

With this Drake interjected, "Aye, I too have a side of me that shall hate to see the day of our departure. But come it shall…" his words trailing off in sort of a melancholy way.

Continuing Geoffrey brought to the fore one of his larger concerns, "the ship is now a good two feet lower in the water. Rough seas will awash the lower gun ports. To prevent this one of the men has made some form of a sealer or wedging from the sap of these trees. He calls a "gasket" or something like that. It seems to work pretty good too. But I don't like the notion of bein' out to sea far from land an havin' to rely on's it."

"The weight of the treasure bring us down?"

"Aye and all the trimmin's and such. We have probably slowed by three or four knots too, I might add. Not good if we's to near the Spanish. I's sure they's figured out by now that it's was us."

"Aye, my friend. And speed is our chief weapon."

"Aye and we could be an easy target as low as we be."

Slapping his friend on the shoulder, Drake responded to these expressions of fear in his usual way, "well I guess they are going to miss us", laughing off the concerns. "For we are setting a course that should take us far from their holdings and out into uncharted waters to the East."

Walking to the makeshift hatchway of his Captain's temporary home, Geoffrey turned back to look at his Captain. "Sure is a shame we's can't off load some of this stuff rights here, or gives it to another to take home whilst we continue. That's way we's won't be so low."

Shaking his head, Geoffrey departed allowing his last words to hang with Drake like a low cloud of smoke from an adjacent campfire.

"Intriguing thought" mused Drake. "I must spend some time with that one."

Annexing the land for England in the name of *Nova Albion* or "New England" invoking the former verbiage for England from the 12th century. This term for England was thought to have been a derivative of the Druid belief in Avalon, the final resting-place of the legendary Arthur. Once again the crew set sail to complete their journey. Leaving behind only a small brass plaque as evidence of their stay.

The Famous Voyage also states Drake so named the land for the white cliffs... He called it New Albion in honor of his own country England, which in ancient times had been called Albion because of the white cliffs and the coast where it was first discovered.

Drake's adventurous life was filled with many accomplishments. He played a major role in the destruction and defeat of the mighty Spanish Armada. This helped England to create a great empire in the New World. He also became the first Englishman to circumnavigate the globe.